HOW TO LIVE WITH A
WOMAN
... and still watch football

BY MICHAEL POWELL

First published in 2005 in Great Britain by Robson Books, The
Chrysalis Building, Bramley Road, London W10 6SP

An imprint of Chrysalis Books Group plc

First published in 2004 by Gusto Company AS
Copyright © 2004, 2005 Gusto Company AS

THE RIGHT OF MICHAEL POWELL TO BE IDENTIFIED AS THE
AUTHOR OF THIS WORK HAS BEEN ASSERTED BY HIM IN
ACCORDANCE WITH THE COPYRIGHT, DESIGNS AND PATENTS ACT

THE AUTHOR HAS MADE EVERY REASONABLE EFFORT TO CONTACT
ALL COPYRIGHT HOLDERS. ANY ERRORS THAT MAY HAVE
OCCURED ARE INADVERTENT AND ANYONE WHO FOR ANY REASON
HAS NOT BEEN CONTACTED IS INVITED TO WRITE TO THE
PUBLISHERS SO THAT A FULL ACKNOWLEDGMENT MAY BE MADE IN
SUBSEQUENT EDITIONS OF THIS WORK.
BRITISH LIBRARY CATALOGUING IN PUBLICATION DATA
A CATALOGUE RECORD FOR THIS TITLE IS AVAILABLE FROM THE
BRITISH LIBRARY.
1 86105 868 3

Illustrated by Greg Paprocki
Original Idea: James Tavendale
Original Design: Bulle Visjon
Original Cover Design: SEE Design
Printed by SNP Leefung, China

INTRODUCTION

Women. Can't live with 'em, but if you do, make sure you've got two TVs.

....

Here's the bad news. If you've got this far you're probably not an Alpha Male. What he does best is sleeping with lots of different partners, having one-night stands and copping off with more than his fair share of beautiful women. He's more of a joy rider than a careful owner.

I'm not an Alpha Male. Can't stand them actually – all that stubbly decisiveness, cleft chinnage and dissolute animal magnetism. But that doesn't mean I don't steal a few of their tricks. The difference is, I play for keeps and that's why I've written this book – an owner's manual for the discerning male who aims to keep the same partner for a considerable mileage. It's for those of us whose self-esteem is underpinned by more than the fleeting thrill of casual sex, expense accounts and the quest for world domination.

Living with a woman is just like football; it requires perseverance, stamina, self-denial, compromise and shin pads. However, it pays to break the rules from time to time. In Mexico in 1986, Diego Maradona's 'Hand of God' was the precursor to arguably the greatest World Cup goal of all time, after he ran from his own half, dribbled around six England players and then nudged in a low ten-yarder.

If you want to be El Pibe de Oro in your home, you've got to grab life by the balls – or at the very least knock them in a favourable direction with the back of your left hand. You won't find happiness by being bullied in the name of The New Man. Believe it or not, I am living proof that it is possible to cohabit with a female while indulging multifarious obsessions, drinking lots of beer and enjoying mind-blowing sex, every day of the week.

Don't get me wrong. I wouldn't be without my missus, but I'm proud to say that I haven't missed a single night out with the lads or even so much as a third division playoff. People often ask me how I have managed to stay with the same person for so long. My response to them is: read the book and find out!

Michael Powell

CONTENTS

Can you handle two of me, baby?

TWENTY RULES FOR LIVING WITH A WOMAN

1. The rules aren't fair and she can change them without notice.

2. Never answer her questions with a grunt. Men know that a grunt means, 'Shut up, I'm trying to watch the game'. Women can't speak grunt. However, they are fluent in pout and sigh.

3. Always take her seriously, even when she's making a right tit of herself.

4. Do as much of the cooking as you can, but always let her believe that she is a better cook than you are.

5. There should only be one pair of jugs in each household. If you start growing 'man-boobs', reduce your alcohol consumption and lower your body mass index.

6. Despite the fact that her breasts are subject to joint ownership, don't refer to them as baps, jugs, norks or use military euphemisms such as bazookas or rockets.

7. Don't assume PMS is the cause of her bad mood, even though it usually is (see page 106).

8. Women can think, breathe and talk at the same time. If she's not talking it doesn't mean she's thinking or taking a breath; it means she's in a bad mood.

9. Get used to fetching her stuff. All the time.

#

The rules aren't fair and she can change them without notice.

10. Always notice when she's had a haircut. If you suspect she's been to the hairdressers, but you're not sure, tell her that her hair looks great.

11. Always let her have the first and last slice of anything.

12. Always let her have a bite of your slice because she'll say it will taste different, even though it won't.

13. If she tells you 'I've never met anyone like you,' it's not necessarily a compliment.

14. Don't expect her to like Britney Spears, Christina Aguilera or Marilyn Manson.

15. Never use the words 'tuna' and 'vagina' in the same sentence.

16. When she says she loves a man with a sense of humour, she doesn't necessarily mean your sense of humour.

Never use the words 'tuna' and 'vagina' in the same sentence.

17. She will expect you to cheer her up whenever she is depressed, but don't presume anything you do will work.

18. She will always assume you are bigger pervert than you really are.

19. She will want you to compliment her all the time, but don't expect her to believe you.

20. If you say something that can be taken two ways, she'll always find a personal insult in there somewhere.

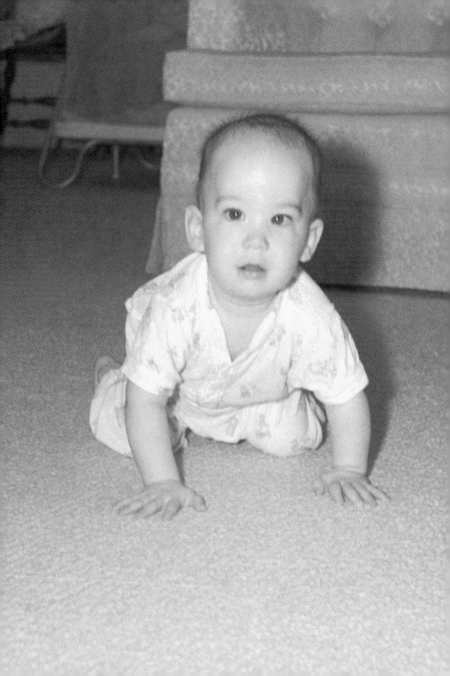

How to Keep
Her Faithful

**There's an old-fashioned view of
monogamy that to ensure a woman's
fidelity you should keep her barefoot
and pregnant. Can this be true?**

....

Monogamy is very rare in the animal kingdom. The
exception being our feathered friends. The term
'love-birds' has arisen with very good reason. About
ninety per cent of birds are monogamous and this is
because, while the female sits on the eggs or tends
to the chicks, she relies on the male to forage for
food. He sometimes travels ball-breaking distances
to bring back tidbits for his brood. In the animal
kingdom, it seems that parenthood is largely a
matter of snack food provision and preventing the
young from becoming the next course on someone
else's menu.

By comparison, monogamy amongst mammals is
rare. Only about five per cent are monogamous.
This is all thanks to those wonderful mammalian
assets: breasts. Female mammals can suckle their
young so they are less dependent on their men folk
to bring in the bacon.

There's a lesson here guys. You don't need to earn
lots of money to be a good father or partner.
Material security is rarely a factor in keeping

women faithful. Rejoice. Shout it from the rooftops of your tiny houses you middle-to-low income males. Why do you think one of the most popular chick flicks of all time is *It's A Wonderful Life*?

Next time you're considering staying late at the office, let the thought of her heaving bosom draw you swiftly home. It's no accident that Capitalism sexualises the mammary glands in order to blind us to their primary function – to sustain life (and to cushion your face after a hard day). Because she has her own children's restaurant under her jumper, a woman is far more likely to leave a rich man who is a feckless father than a poor man who is profoundly involved in the social, emotional and intellectual development of his children. In the developed world, human monogamy is not about survival or even material comforts.

If you want to keep your woman faithful, forget about how much you earn, or putting in a sixty-hour week. The nutritional needs of your children can be met with relative ease. Put quite simply, if you don't make the grade as a provider, your ankle-biters won't starve to death.

So that must mean women stay with men for another reason. Human offspring require more intensive social care than just about any animal on the planet. So it's in a woman's interests to stick around only if her man is being a good father. Once she's got kids nothing else is more important to her. The single most effective way of keeping her faithful is this:

Get her pregnant, have lots of children and be an excellent father. Go forth and multiply.

How to Be Assertive

If you want to be the sort of strong-minded male that drives women wild, study Austin Powers. Why? Because he is a rare thing, an Alpha male who's not afraid of relationships. He's honest, optimistic, goofy and has lots of cool stuff. OK, that's four things right there: let's take them in order. Groovy, baby.

Honesty
Be honest about what you want and how you feel about her. How can you bend her to your will if she doesn't know what you want? Express your thoughts, feelings and beliefs directly without putting her down. This means respecting her needs as well as your own and telling her when she's talking bollocks.

Optimism
Powerful men inspire others with the strength of their personality, which usually springs from a faith in humanity and a genuine interest in others. For all his shortcomings, Austin is a sexy man to a host of lovely ladies because he gives people his full attention and has a generosity of spirit – an almost naïve optimism that energises

himself and others. Encourage her to share your beliefs by selling them with passion and watch your mojo rising.

Always make her feel totally shag-a-delic

BEING GOOFY

Don't take yourself too seriously. A self-deprecating joke told with confidence is more accessible and disarming than the usual male competitive put-down. 'We don't laugh any more,' is a common complaint among many women. Don't lose that playful spirit.

PROTECT YOUR STUFF

The woman in your life must respect your worldly possessions. All guys have them. Alpha guys have more accoutrements than most and they're not afraid to defend them. That means, if you're living together, your paraphernalia take pride of place – be it your DVD collection, your lava lamps or your mixing decks. They shouldn't live in a back room – they need to be on display. The first thing a woman will try to do is banish your belongings to a rarely used part of the house then introduce girly clutter like candles, potpourri, baskets full of fir cones, wooden dolphins, photographs and even more candles. If you're not living together, she'll try her best to borrow and proceed to break most of your possessions.

MAKE HER FEEL SEXY

Always make her feel totally shag-a-delic. How do you do that? Constantly tell her she's looking 'shag-a-delic'. Austin does it because he knows that no matter what faults he may have, so long as he keeps giving her those special compliments, she will forgive him most of his indiscretions. Oh behave!

Signs She's Getting Lazy

She can only get half as much into the dishwasher as you can – that's forgivable – a woman's lack of spatial awareness is always endearing (except when she's vacuuming in front of the TV or driving a car). But the moment she looks up at you, flutters her eyelids and purrs, 'Will you do it for me?', it may be a warning that she's getting lazy. Here are some others:

....

1. She begins to criticise you for things you have done since the dawn of time, like picking your nose, farting and watching sport on telly.
2. She starts nagging you about things she should have done herself, like taking the rubbish out, putting the toilet seat down and sorting out the children at the weekend – like when do you get your break?
3. You can't remember a time when she had just the one stomach and wore trousers that weren't made of spandex.
4. She's growing a moustache that Burt Reynolds would be proud of. Her armpits, legs and bikini line haven't seen a razor for months. Beware! She may claim that your lager tits make you evens,

SHE RARELY WAKES UP ANY MORE DURING SEX.

despite the fact that her 'tache would qualify her for membership of the handlebar club. But guys have been drinking beer for centuries and there are no accounts of medieval darts players being chased out of their villagers for being lady-boy witches.

5. She starts getting spiritual and doing yoga – just another excuse to lie on the floor and do bugger all.

6. You regularly run out of clean underwear.

7. She rarely wakes up any more during sex.

8. You get a kebab on your way home from the pub every night because you know she won't have stayed up to cook you anything. She used to bake her own bread, and make you gourmet meals every night. Now, the only time she even opens a tin is to feed the cat.

Don't be unreasonable. It's not her fault. Clearly, laziness has many manifestations, but fortunately it only has one cause: amnesia. Women simply forget their duty, the importance of gender roles and, most important of all, the needs of a man. It's your duty to help her improve her memory.

First off, remind her that it was a woman who invented the dishwasher, to liberate her sisterhood from the drudgery of washing-up. Buy her some chocolate-covered almonds and suggest she takes a B vitamin supplement. Get her to memorise post-war FA Cup winners – anything so long as it restores those atrophied neural connections.

With time, she'll recall the unspoken contract you agreed at the start of your relationship, namely, that you will remain monogamous in return for regular feeding and sex with a slim and attractive woman who accepts and loves you for who you are.

So long as you keep your side of the bargain, it isn't unreasonable to expect certain minimum requirements; but leaving a note on the fridge saying 'Sex – tonight at 8.30pm' just won't cut it.

How to Live With a Woman... and Still Watch Football

It's Saturday afternoon. The match starts in twenty minutes. You've invited six of your drinking buddies round to watch and they're already trounced after spending the morning in the pub. One of them has been sick in the kitchen sink. You've told her not to bother clearing it up – you'll do it later. She's sulking and wondering when she can have her life back.

....

Watching football and drinking alcohol is one of life's greatest pleasures and it needn't be a male reserve. Unfortunately it's one that many women forfeit, not because they wouldn't enjoy it, but because they have never been invited into this largely male arena.

First off, explain the rules. How can you expect her to enthuse about something she doesn't understand? Find a quiet time together to watch an important game you've recorded on video. Make it civilised and inviting. Light some candles, turn down the lights and open a bottle of wine (no lager allowed), then cuddle on the sofa. You'll already know the score, so you won't be tempted to punch the air or swear at the TV. At first it won't matter if she's not interested so long as she's enjoying your company. The important thing is you've broken the ice and got her to watch, while you explain the rules and nibble her earlobes.

Your knowledge of your favourite sport is bound to be impressive and that can be intimidating. How can she ever hope to catch up? If she's asking questions then answer them without being patronising. It's inevitable that there's plenty she won't know about the sport – even the simplest thing. Have patience. It will take time, but as her knowledge of the sport grows along with her appreciation of the skills involved, you'll be amazed at how quickly she transforms from disinterested sulk to one of the lads.

Next, make her aware how skilled the players are. You appreciate how hard it is to dribble past three defenders, but she won't. So take her, a ball and a picnic down the park and have a kick around. If you choose a glorious summer's day and make it a memorable romantic experience, she'll begin to associate the beautiful game with intimacy, and feel less excluded on match days. She may even discover she loves playing and announce her intention to join a female league.

The other thing to remember about women is that they are relationship oriented. They're less interested in tactics than the personalities taking part. So if you can get her interested in them you're halfway there. For instance saying, 'there's Thierry Henry, he's a world-class striker' will leave her cold, but pointing out that he's that gorgeous guy in the Renault Clio 'va va voom' advert will pique her interest. Encourage her to tell you which players she fancies.

In the World Cup there were more female supporters in Brazil than male ones. These are women who have been involved in the football culture and haven't been made to feel excluded from it and that's as much to do with the country that you're brought up in as anything else.

If your woman was doing something that was exclusively female, such as having a Victoria's Secret party, you might secretly like to take part but you'd feel like you weren't welcome. It's the same with sport.

Eventually you may even get her shotgunning six packs of beer, and, who knows, once you've got her interested in one sport you can move on to the real hard-core male domains like Turkish oil wrestling or bullfighting. Good luck!

PERSUADING HER TO AGREE TO A THREESOME

Can you handle two of me, baby?

If you want something, honesty isn't always the best policy. But if you don't ask you don't get, right? You have to work up to these things. If you just spring it on her as a *fait accompli* she'll think you're just after a bit of cheap titillation rather than genuinely seeking to take your relationship to a deeper and more meaningful level!

. . . .

There are many different approaches you can take. Choose whichever of these four approaches best suits your situation.

1. LOVEY-DOVEY
'I love you so much. I love all of you. Everything about you.

I can't get enough of you. Gee, I wish there were two of you. I'd be twice as happy if I could bring pleasure to two of you – it would double the meaning in my life. But, alas, you are unique. There is no one like you. But what if, say, we found someone who was a bit like you – a woman I mean, who could, maybe, join in and er, pretend to be you. If you feel uncomfortable with that, then she could just come as herself. While I was with her I'd be thinking of you – I'd be thinking twice as much about you. So what do you say? There's actually a woman in work I know who would be just perfect. Shall I give her a ring now . . . ?'

2. TERMINAL ILLNESS

'Darling, you know how I'm cursed by this dreadful terminal illness? Well, I was wondering if, before my next dose of debilitating medication, and while I still have the energy . . . there's something I'd like to see before I die. It would be a dream come true. Will you help me to see my dream before God takes me? Will you wear a twelve-inch strap-on and roger another woman while I watch . . . cough . . . cough . . . it just might help to ease this terrible pain . . .'

3. PLAY HARD TO GET

'Darling . . . you know that idea you had last week about inviting one of your hot friends to join us in a threesome . . . well I'm not sure it's such a good idea after all.'

4. ASK FOR THE EARTH

Ask for more than you want and you'll get what you really want. Suggest an orgy with six of her mates. She'll feel relieved after she negotiates you down to a cosy threesome.

Gee, I wish there were two of you.

LEAVING THE TOILET SEAT UP

When did women get to decide the position of the toilet seat? Why don't they leave it up? Why do they believe that peeing sitting down is the only way for them?

....

Have they ever considered that just as men hog the best jobs, the highest salaries and the remote control, that women will never have equal rights until they can pee anywhere? Men don't need a seat. Hell, they don't even need a toilet.

The benefits of standing far outweigh the risks. Men never have to queue. We don't need to sit on or hover above a disease-ridden public toilet seat. It's the environmentally friendly way to urinate. Men's urinals use less water to flush and shaking instead of wiping saves millions of trees worldwide every year. Standing shoulder to shoulder while peeing gives us a sense of community (as long as you obey the code and never look anywhere but straight ahead). Women are expected to hide away in a private and often filthy cubicle.

And the biggest myth of all? That men are actually any good at it. They are useless, even though they act as if pissing on their shoes, the walls and the floor is their birthright.

Three more reasons why peeing standing up is good for her:

1. She can flush while she pees and try to beat the flush

2. She can be sick at the same time

3. She can write her name in fresh snow

For further information on how to pee standing up, direct her to:
www.restrooms.org/standing.html

How to Handle
Her Nagging

'Have you listened to a word I've just said? Why didn't you call to tell me you'd be late home? Why didn't you bring me a cup too? Why do you always only think of yourself . . .?'

....

Sounds familiar? Why is it that one day your woman will greet you with a smile when you come rolling back from the pub with beer breath and chilli sauce on your trousers and then the next time she's on your case before you've even had time to take a leak? Why is a fart funny one minute and gross the next?

BARK
BARK!

You're going to have to accept that women are unpredictable, which means that their reactions are generally beyond your control. So don't go changing your behaviour all the time to please her. You'll end up having nothing left to change and chances are you'll still get nagged.

Accept that women are always going to nag. They saw their dads getting nagged by their mums and grew up thinking it's the natural thing to do. They watch shows like *Roseanne* and *Friends* where the men are put down all the time. So how are you going to deal with it?

27

First you need to determine what kind of nag you are dealing with. They generally fall into three categories:

THE SILENT NAG

She doesn't tell you why she's annoyed with you. In fact, she won't talk to you at all. She expects you to figure it out all by yourself and will work herself into a mute rage just because you can't read her mind.

If you respond to a silent nag by asking what's wrong, you are playing into her hands. But don't give her the silent treatment, since silent naggers can never be beaten at their own game.

The only way to end the stalemate is to bite your lip and apologise. If she tries to trump you by asking you what you are apologising for, say, 'for not learning to understand you and your feelings better'. She can't argue with that.

INDIRECT NAG

When she asks a question like 'Are you going to have a shave today?', if you don't walk into the bathroom and reach for a blade, you risk being on the receiving end of a full frontal nag.

Indirect nags are time bombs that can be diffused by plain communication. Ask her to clarify her feelings: 'Are you saying that you'd like me to have a shave?' If she says 'Yes', then at least you know where she stands and you can counter with your own feelings. If she is vague or evasive, then make her be specific.

NON-STOP NAG

The opposite of the silent nag, the non-stop nagger

doesn't stop banging on about the same thing. She'll usually choose the moment you're watching your favourite TV programme, so she can also nag you for not paying attention.

Say something. Anything. Talk to her. Thinking in silence is not something women understand. Women often think aloud by bouncing their ideas off each other. Men tend to think silently but if you say nothing she'll think you haven't been listening.

Communication is the key to combating nagging. Listen and talk and, who knows, if you show real understanding, a nag might just end in a shag.

BE AWARE: THINKING IN SILENCE IS NOT SOMETHING WOMEN UNDERSTAND!

Keeping Two
Girlfriends

Monogamy is like walking the wrong way up an Olympic luge. You need immense willpower, fearless commitment and blind hope you won't get knocked over by four men in Kevlar body suits. OK, the analogy doesn't bear over-analysis. Suffice to say, monogamy goes against the natural flow of what is hardwired into our loins: men are genetically programmed to indulge in a little binary coupling.

· ·

When buses come in threes, you can only ride one of them. Fortunately it's different with women, which means you can score gorgeous girlfriend number two while still dating voracious girlfriend number one. What next?

The most important rule is DON'T GET CAUGHT. Women do the weirdest things when you play around. You don't need two demented chicks hacking the arms off your Armani suit and attempting nocturnal circumcision.

Be aware that double-dipping will take up twice as much of your time and energy. You'll get extra

RULE

#1

DON'T
GET
CAUGHT!

#

helpings of the good bits (twice the boobage). This would at first glance seem to be a simple equation even if you're really bad at maths, but be prepared to put up with twice as much aggro as well.
You can't get away with treating each date as half a better half.

Try to avoid dating women in the same city. You don't want to risk bumping into one while dating the other, which could result in you having to fake severe memory loss.

Always answer your cell phone while on a date. She'll get suspicious if you're ignoring calls. If it's the other woman, ask if you can call her back later.

Date them on different days – women have a better sense of smell than a pack of wolves – they'll know when you've been with someone else.

Try to appear as under the thumb as possible. If another woman flirts with you while you are with one of your girlfriends, fake embarrassment and look really overwhelmed. They'll never suspect you've got the balls to cheat on them.

Play away from home. Meet at neutral territory or her place. If you bring them home you risk leaving evidence – hairs on pillows, make-up traces on a towel, a bottle of champagne in the bin.

It's inevitable that you'll have to tell some lies – but keep them simple. If you make your excuses too specific you'll find them hard to remember and she'll get suspicious. Truth is often much simpler than a lie, so keep your lies simple and vague.

If by some stroke of fortune, one of your women says she's OK with an open relationship, don't rush in and confess all. She's probably trying to trick you and you'll be woken up the next morning by a female Edward Scissorhands. Anyway, how can you respect a woman that accepts two-timing? Low self-esteem is such a turn-off.

When you've found the one you want to spend the rest of your life with, don't even look at another woman. What are you trying to do, ruin your life? Double dating increases your chances of finding what you're looking for – a bit like using a search engine on the Internet. But once you've found it, stop browsing.

It's strange, he's always so tired...

How to Get Her to Lose Weight

If your girlfriend has let herself go during the last few years and has put on over twenty pounds how can you tell her to buff up without offending?

....

Never tell a woman to lose weight. You never tell a woman she is fat. Even if she is thin she'll still think she's fat, so pointing it out will just make her hit you and then the refrigerator.

Think about it. You want her to feel good about herself all the time. If she's put on a bit of extra weight, take it as a compliment. It means she feels relaxed with you. There's a lot of truth in the saying that putting a ring on a woman's finger is like pulling the ripcord on a parachute.

But, even if she needs winching out of bed every morning, keep telling her she's beautiful and you'll stand a better chance of getting her to shed those extra pounds.

Treat her being overweight as you both being overweight (which is probably true). Why not start cooking low fat dinners. Tell her you'll take care of the shopping and preparing of meals. Suggest joining a gym together. Watching your

#

Never tell a woman to lose weight!

34

girl work out and get buns of steel will give you real satisfaction.

Try taking at least three or four romantic walks every week. Even better – buy a dog. That will force you both to get some exercise every day.

Hey, looks like all that sex is finally giving results.

Take a good hard look at yourself. Do you still take as much care over your own appearance as you did when you first met? Have you lowered your standards and allowed a few ugly habits to creep in? Does she still make the same effort to look good when you go out together? If not, maybe its time to look at how you might be helping her pile on the pounds.

Be upbeat about things about her that you don't like. If you think she drinks or eats too much, then focus on how much fun you have when she's not drinking or how much fun you both have when you are down at the swimming pool. Being positive makes both of you feel better.

It's the best way to go about it. You have to make sure they feel good about themselves ALL the time.

If none of that works then kick her to the curb and start dating someone with a good figure. She'll have dropped four dress sizes before you can say 'eating disorder'.

How Honest Should You Be?

Honesty is key in a relationship. If you can fake that, you've got it made. Trouble is, most men are rotten liars, so it looks like you're stuck with genuine honesty after all.

....

Honesty is a long term bet. It's a bit like getting a tattoo – painful at first, then addictive and something you may or may not live to regret. It's uncomfortable the moment you reveal secrets early in a relationship – especially if it's something that will hurt her. However, if you can commit to the relationship, most revealed secrets will be things you can look back and tease each other about ten years on.

The question is, when do you start revealing your innermost secrets? It's a great feeling to know that your partner knows everything about you and still loves you but that's not a place you can get to in a matter of weeks.

There are four types of personal information. First there's the must-tell facts. For example, you've got a sexually transmitted disease. A sure-fire way to save embarrassment is to go and get it sorted out the moment you find 'that' girl. If for any reason you can't, confess this right at the start. But if you've got a third nipple or used to have a crush on William Shatner, save it. If you stand to inherit a few million, that's a good one to keep for later.

Second, there's the stuff that you may be proud of but which won't impress her – like the eighty women you've slept with. Keep that one locked away until she feels totally secure with you.

Thirdly, there's those things that make you vulnerable, like how you felt when your dog died or how good your mum smells. That sort of personal info is wetter than a fish's bikini, but it will show her you've got a sensitive soul. (However, telling her all about 'the one' who broke your heart, then sobbing in her arms for two hours won't make her feel very special.)

Finally there's the real big secrets like your gender reassignment or the guy you buried under your patio seventeen years ago . . . you're on your own there fella.

If you've been unfaithful, but you don't want to tell her because you're afraid you'll lose her, then you're lying to yourself and her. If you were afraid of losing her you wouldn't have had a fling in the first place. You are actually afraid of hurting her feelings.

What she doesn't know can't hurt her, right? Well, if you really see a future together you can't keep a secret like that forever. Guilt is an unwelcome third party in a relationship and you're more likely to have another affair if you don't confess. It will hang over you and destroy any great moments you share. If you don't feel guilty, then you're still missing out by keeping her at a distance.

Be honest about what you want from a relationship.
If you only want casual, uncomplicated sex, then it's
unfair to lead her on by letting her think there's
more to it than that.

Finally, when she asks about her appearance, lie.
And make it good.

If he says
over 100, then
I'll lie and say
only 50...

How to Score
Points with Her

It's quite simple. Do things she likes and you gain points. Do things that irritate her and you lose them. You get no points for performing chores that she takes for granted like leaving the toilet seat down or taking out the rubbish.

Open a window or light a match after farting

-2

Stop farting until so much noxious gas builds up in your intestines that you have to be rushed into hospital for an emergency procedure

+20

You switch off the TV when she wants to talk

0

Leave the room to fart

0

Make sure there's petrol in the car

+1

Ask directions when you're lost

0

Load the dish-washer every time you use something

+1

Reload the dishwasher because she's done it wrong

-2

You remove a spider from the bath

+1

You remove a spider from the bath and flush it down the toilet

+2

You pretend there's a spider on her shoulder

-15

You buy her a replacement without bothering to take it apart

+5

You remove a spider from the bath, walk five hundred yards away from the house, bury it six feet underground and fill the hole with concrete

+10

You take something apart and fix it

+1

You take something apart then can't put it back together, leaving the components all over the living room floor

-5

Wash your hands after going to the toilet

0

Remember her birthday

0

Hold her hand in public

0

You double the capacity of your single-visit salad bowl by placing cucumber slices round the edge then spend twenty minutes filling it so full you have to walk slowly back to your table grinning with your hand on the top

-10

Take longer to get ready than her

-2

You let her watch TV when you want to talk

0

Say something 'sweet'

+3

Give hugs and kisses at all times

0

Do something 'sweet'

+3

Shave every day

+1

Be especially kind and sensitive when she has PMS

0

When shopping, you go for as many coffee breaks as she wants without complaining you can get free coffee at home

0

Shave when you want sex

-5

Point out she has PMS

-10

You go out to get milk and return only with beer

-10

Restaurant
You pay the bill without checking it

+3

You look at the waitress's cleavage as she bends over to serve you

0

Your partner notices

-10

You come back with beer and milk and a chocolate bar for her

+1

You come back with milk and a chocolate bar for her

+10

You leave her alone while you take an eight-minute dump

-10

Ten Sex Myths You Shouldn't Believe

1. **She can't get pregnant while menstruating**
   There's only one day in a month that a woman can get pregnant, but since sperm can live up to five days, having sex during her period is no guarantee that she won't.

2. **Men can't have multiple orgasms**
   While it is a largely female preserve (about 30% of women have experienced them), some lucky guys have reported having repeated orgasms without losing their stiffies.

3. **An average penis is 6 inches long**
   The average pan handle is 5.1 inches, but the average flaccid penis is a mere 3.5 inches.

4. **Women lose interest in sex after menopause and have difficulty having an orgasm**
   Menopause does not significantly affect the ability to orgasm, the orgasmic experience itself or a woman's libido. A menopausal woman is only likely to be off her sex if she and her partner have got into a sexual rut.

5. **There's no such thing as a G-Spot**
   Dr Ruth Westheimer doesn't think it exists, but it most definitely does. It's situated on the back wall of the vagina between the opening and the cervix.

One condom is enough!

6. **Men have a higher sex drive than women**
Research has proved time and time again that men and women share sex drives of equal or near-equal intensity. If you're feeling oversexed, you're not making her feel special enough to get her in the mood – it has nothing to do with her baseline sex drive.

7. **Two condoms are better than one**
Doubling up your johnnies actually makes you less safe, because the condoms will rub together and increase the chance of splitting.

8. **'Blue balls' is something men make up**
There's a name for it: vasocongestion, and it's very real. When you're aroused the blood flow to your genitals greatly increases and then decreases again after orgasm. If you don't ejaculate you may end up in severe discomfort, but it's not harmful.

9. **Women can't ejaculate**
Yes they can, if you stimulate their G-Spot (see point 5), releasing a quantity of clear watery fluid from the urethra. Until the 1950s, ejaculating women were considered to be suffering from incontinence and were offered surgery to 'cure' them.

10. **Your parents have only had sex five times**
They used to and probably still shag like rabbits. Don't fall prey to the rumour that you'll get little to no sex as you get older. A healthy libido can be maintained for many years by mixing it up in the bedroom and making her feel special all the time.

44

How to Keep Her Low Maintenance

What exactly is a low-maintenance partner? She's a person who respects your three most precious resources: time, money and emotions. If your woman demands large portions of any of these commodities, she may be high maintenance (HM) and more trouble than she's worth.

....

Some say that LM women are born not made. For example, if she hates shopping but loves taking romantic walks on the beach, or if she's a Buddhist (enjoys her own company, eschews material possessions and is fairly chilled out). Unfortunately there aren't that many hot Buddhist chicks around.

Check out which one of these descriptions most fits your beatch:

Poodle (HM)
Spends most of her time at the hairdressers and the manicurist is always on call. She has so many shoes that Victoria Beckham phones her for advice. She has four credit cards and they're all yours.

She has so many shoes that Victoria Beckham phones her for advice.

Dalmatian (HM)

Nervous and highly strung, she relies upon you to boost her self-esteem. She sees you as her protector and you spend the whole time wrapping her in cotton wool. At first you were attracted to her fragile femininity but now you're seeing spots.

Irish Terrier (HM)

Once she has her teeth into you she won't let go. You belong to her and her jealous streak makes your life hell if you so much as look at another woman. Dating a terrier is a painful experience that will leave you scarred for life.

Labrador (LM)

Likes nothing better than staying in with a take-away and a video. Simple pleasures keep her happy like snuggling up to you in front of the fire. Does have a tendency to gain weight and leave hair in the bath plug.

Saint Bernard (LM)

She's always coming to your rescue and you can rely on her in a crisis. She may secretly complain to her friends that you are high maintenance, so don't get too dependent on her ability to fix your problems.

German Shepherd (LM)

Assertive and confident, she knows what she wants. However, you need lots of energy and charisma to match her pace. She's so headstrong she might look elsewhere to meet her carnal and intellectual needs.

Identify the spaces in your life that she is invading and take the necessary action:

EMOTIONS

She's needy and clingy and always wants your approval. She sulks for days if you don't bring her little gifts and tell her how much you love her.

Boost her self-confidence by playing along with her excessive demands until she settles down and realises she doesn't have to hog the limelight to get your attention. If that doesn't work you can always kick her in to touch and find a woman who respects herself and doesn't need a psychiatrist for a partner.

MONEY

She arrives home with another pair of Gucci boots and throws them in the wardrobe with the other three pairs she has never worn.

Cut up your credit cards and tell her that her debts are her own responsibility. She's probably only staying with you for your mullah, so get out, unless you're a professional footballer who owns an oil company.

TIME

She wants to spend every minute of the day with you, and can't understand it when you want to go out with the lads or do something on your own.

She's a relationship junkie who hates her own company. Stand your ground, and, while a little compromise is healthy, make sure you don't lose your right to you-time.

She arrives home with another pair of Gucci boots and throws them in the wardrobe.

Getting Sex
on Demand

A relationship is like a fire. Once lit you must stoke it and throw on more wood at regular intervals. Do you know how to seduce your woman? Do you know what seduction is?

....

Her idea of seduction will be very different from yours. We've all heard jokes about how men like to dive straight in without paying proper attention to the rest of a woman's body, not to mention her mind. Let's hope that you're more sophisticated than that.

How often do you make non-sexual physical contact – stroking a cheek, holding hands or kissing her gently? The distinction here is physical contact that shows affection and makes her feel loved without the subtext of 'I want sex'. You've got to make her feel physically desirable all day while at the same time keeping quiet about your urge to throw her onto the kitchen table and hump her brains out.

Actually, the word seduction gets in the way, because it already suggests a power imbalance, with one party trying to win over the other. It's much more useful to think more in terms of an invitation.

If you invite her to have intimate relations with you, this mental shift can be enough to change both your attitudes. It allows for greater communication and respect and is based on the premise that she has a choice.

Also, it takes the pressure off you to allow the invitation to be declined – you won't feel like it was 'your job' to get her in the mood. The more you lighten up about her declining, the more success you will have. If she doesn't feel like it, it is no reflection on you.

Above all you must give sex the respect that it demands. It must be an expression of love – deep and intimate. Lovemaking is about honouring the essence of each other while pleasuring each other's bodies. If you treat sex with respect then your attitude will bring you both to new levels of spiritual intimacy.

Respect me!

ARE YOU A LAZY LOVER?

Lost the spark? Can't be bothered to haul your ass into bed for another night of passion? We all go through phases where sex seems like too much hassle, but some men are just plain lazy in the bedroom and don't put nearly enough effort into their love life. Check out these warning signs to see if you're a torpid cupid.

. . . .

1. You think that Mutual Orgasm is actually an insurance company.
2. You never use a condom because the packaging is just too darn fiddly.
3. You always keep your clothes on.
4. You like being tied up: it allows you to have a good rest.
5. You fall asleep while masturbating.
6. You use a megaphone when you want to have noisy sex.
7. You think a sex aid is a charity.
8. You like S&M because the pain keeps you awake during sex.
9. The cat falls asleep at the foot of the bed during a hot session.
10. Your heart rate decreases during sex.

GORDON'S VIAGRA-ONLY DIET KEPT SUE ON HER TOES

11. You call it French Kissing, while she calls it mouth to mouth.
12. She suddenly starts pounding on your ribcage and then administers 'French Kissing'.
13. You get your climax when the Meals on Wheels arrive.
14. During sex you can actually make time go backwards.
15. The only time you bring her to climax is when you have a seizure.
16. You take Viagra just to stay awake.
17. A multiple orgasm is three climaxes, three weeks running.

The best cure for a flagging libido is lots of sex. The more sex you have, the better shape you're in and the more energy you'll have. Intercourse is fantastic aerobic exercise and burns six calories a minute. The more energy you have the higher your libido. Now that's one vicious circle you don't want to break.

Getting Away with Annoying Habits

Men seem to have a dazzling collection of irritating habits but it's a constant battle to defend our right to perform them at will in female company. They are a constant source of frustration and it seems we're always on the receiving end of a habit-related ultimatum.

....

First of all, recognise that habits are normal. You're not the only person in the world who picks his nose, farts, snores or doesn't bother to change the toilet roll, but she'll act like you are.

Secondly, distinguish between habits, character traits and pet peeves. A character trait is a habit that is bound up with your personality and how you see yourself. These are the most difficult habits to break and ones which she may have to accommodate (like your donkey-laugh or the way you suck your teeth when you're thinking). Pet peeves are the easiest to deal with because they are things that just she finds annoying, so you can easily make a case that she is being unreasonable. Finally, recognise the difference between habits that are disgusting and those which are merely annoying.

No woman should be expected to tolerate more than three disgusting habits (these are ones that you wouldn't perform in front of a stranger or a hot woman), so choose your top three and stick with them. Then negotiate on the rest. Write a list together of your respective habits and trade them off. Agree to stop drumming your fingers all the time if she'll stop using your razors to shave her legs. Trade adjusting your tackle in public for her sticking to the point when she's telling a story. Agree to leave the room to fart if she'll stop being a total fruit loop, and so on.

Habit rotation is another strategy. This involves performing specific habits on certain days of the week. This draws less attention to them and lets you get away with more. Avoid compounding habits. This is behaviour where a modifier either immediately before or afterwards magnifies the irritation factor. For example, either clearing the area for a fart or laughing about it afterwards, or sneezing loudly then showing her the contents of your handkerchief.

If she isn't willing to compromise and you own a cat, you can always use the 'feline defence'. Point out that little Whiskers has more anti-social fixations than Charles Manson. You never jump on the keyboard when she's trying to work, kick litter on the floor or dig your fingernails into her legs to stop yourself from falling off the sofa. You never lie down where she wants to sit, drag in headless squirrels from the garden or eat the houseplants and then throw up all over the living room. If women can tolerate that much crap from an animal, it's time they cut men some slack.

FAAART

HOW TO COPE WITH
HER BORING FRIENDS

**You've planned a cosy twosome: you
think maybe you'll take her to see the
latest Quentin Tarantino movie followed
by a curry and a night of passion. Life
is sweet.**

....

You're looking forward to doing the three
things you love most: watching violence, eating
curries and having sex. Then she drops the
bombshell – you're not going anywhere – you're
staying in remember? She's invited her friends
around to play.

Major change of plan. The girls are coming. But
these aren't just any girls. These are the most
boring people you have ever met in your life. So
what do you do?

The first thing to decide is whether they are in fact
the most tedious group of sentient beings in the
known universe, or if they only seem dull because
you're no longer the centre of attention. If this is
the case, then you'd better salvage what you can
from the evening. If you tolerate them, you'll get
in her good books and you may still end up with
your night of passion, even if you won't get to see
Uma Thurman butchering fifty people with a
Samurai sword.

Can I come and play too?

If you think her friends are boring, chances are you don't think too much of her either. Let's face it, if you had the chance to be with the woman of your dreams for the rest of your life, on condition that you mingle with a few mingers, would you take it or leave it?

Boring really means they're not cool or sexy enough. You don't want to hang around with her lame ugly friends because it emphasises how lame and ugly she is too. OK – so maybe you should be with someone else, but don't pass up the chance to get to know her friends – they may know some really hot chicks.

Don't, under any circumstances, get arseholed. Alcohol may temporarily make them appear more interesting, but after ten large glasses of Chardonnay and three hours of their company, you'll be questioning the purpose of your existence on this planet and you'll be checking your watch wondering whether you can slip out for a kebab without anyone noticing. Then, when you go to bed she'll start nagging you for being such a grump. She'll win the argument because she will be more sober than you, and all you'll want to do is sleep. After experiencing the most tedious evening of your entire life, the last thing you want is a row at 1.00am then wake up feeling like you've been eaten by a llama and spat out over a cliff.

BEDTIME, DARLING!

WHEN YOUR FRIENDS HATE HER

When you're dating someone your friends don't get on with, they may, either directly or indirectly, try and do everything in their power to make you see sense. There are three reasons why they might encourage you to strangle her.

....

1. THEY ARE JEALOUS
You're dating a babe whom your friends probably told you was out of your league, but you ignored them and had the presence of mind to ask her out. Now you're dating her and they aren't – they feel cheated and jealous. The only way they can make themselves feel better is to pretend she isn't worth it. There must be something wrong with her if she's dating you, right? Thanks for the support, guys.

2. THEY THINK SHE'S A TROLL
Clearly this is the opposite of being jealous. They feel you could scrape a more attractive mate off the bottom of your shoe and can't bear to see you hooked up with such an ugly witch. She must have you under some weird spell, otherwise you wouldn't look twice at her – so now they think she's manipulative as well as ugly. They only have your interests at heart, but it should only matter to you

if you agree with them. If what they say bothers you, that means you know she's a troll but haven't the guts to admit it to yourself. It's no good dating someone if there's no mutual physical attraction.

3. SHE SUCKS

Your friends will most likely take a dislike to someone who isn't treating you right or is horribly wrong for you. Take this analogy: if you've got a brute of a car then they're not going to tell you to trade it in, but if your car is always breaking down and is high maintenance, they'll advise you to check out other models. Take heed, because they can give you an outside perspective that you're too wrapped up to see. When you're in the driving seat it's easy to ignore the rust under the wheel arches. If she is trying to change you and not loving you for who you are, your friends will be better placed to spot this than you.

It's easy to try to convince yourself that you're happy with your partner because you so badly want the relationship to work that you ignore the fact that something basic is broken or missing. If a relationship is making you unhappy, good friends will be the first to notice, even if you haven't told them. It can be hard to hear, but it may be a sign that you aren't being honest with yourself.

Getting Her to Pick Up After You

Training your woman to clear up your mess as well as her own is not as big a challenge as you might think. For a start, women still do more housework than men, so you're probably off to a head start already, unless she's got you completely whipped.

....

Still, if the hours of slavery she puts in aren't adequate, you might consider some of these tactics:

1. Give her positive reinforcement whenever she is doing a household chore. When she is washing-up, come up behind her, wrap your arms around her waist and say 'Mmm, you look so sexy with your hands in a bowl of soapy water.' She may laugh, but if you're lucky, her subconscious may well be associating doing the washing-up with being sexy and attractive.

Try using this technique in many different situations – while she's hanging out the washing or doing the ironing. And be sure to remind her to have a nice, crisp shirt ready for the morning.

Soon she'll be dressing up for you. She'll be taking out the rubbish wearing a babydoll, she'll clean the oven in silk underwear and get a thrill of erotic pleasure from picking up your wet, smelly towel from the bathroom floor. Because all the time you have been sending her powerful messages that domesticity equals femininity – just like in the good old days when men ate Brylcream and women had sore knees and callused hands.

2. Get her pregnant. Her nesting instinct will override any attempts to house train you. She'll be steam cleaning the carpets and scrubbing the kitchen floor 24/7.

3. Invite her mother around when you're away on a business trip. She comes from a generation that knew that the woman's place was to clean and will expect the same high standards from her daughter – who will tidy up the whole house before her arrival.

4. Leave chocolate treats inside the fingers of her marigolds. Even though she's elbow deep in suds, the intravenous chocolate-under-the-nails rush is a powerful reinforcer.

5. Every time there is a programme on the Discovery channel about microbes and how many million skin mites there are in your carpet, watch it together. Whereas we men recognise that parasites and bugs are an invisible fact of life, women seem to have an automatic guilt response. She'll be up and vacuuming before the first ad break.

6. In the end, division of labour around the house is down to effective communication. If she isn't doing more than her fair share, then you may have to resort to good old-fashioned shouting.

Going on Holiday Together

There's more to going on holiday together than turning up at the airport on the right day. It means doing everything together – including planning.

....

It's tempting to let her shove a few holiday brochures under your nose, to which you say 'Oh, that's nice – whatever'. But planning the holiday together should be fun and relaxing and make you both excited about what's to come.

Be honest about the sort of holiday you want. Don't agree to lie on a beach for two weeks if you would rather be white-water rafting or getting your stomach pumped at the Oktoberfest in Munich. Find a compromise where both of you can be happy.

Pack your own suitcase – don't leave it all to her – she'll choose clothes that you hate and she'll forget to pack any underwear. But don't forget to leave a little romantic surprise in her suitcase – some sexy lingerie or jewellery.

Holidays should be relaxing, so don't put pressure on yourself or your partner by having unrealistic expectations. Don't rely on external factors to have fun and relax together. If the weather isn't up to scratch, don't let it spoil your holiday. You're away from home, away from the routine – have fun together – there aren't any rules so, as long as you don't have preconceptions about the holiday, you can be flexible.

Build in some time apart. It's OK to spend time apart on holiday – that means she can check out the museums while you kick back in the cocktail bar. Then arrange to meet up at a special restaurant in the evening – you'll have plenty to talk about and you will appreciate each other's company even more.

Meet new people. It takes the focus off the two of you trying to satisfy each other.

Plan your budget before the holiday, so that you aren't preoccupied about how your overdraft is increasing back home. Otherwise when she suggests dining at that smart restaurant, you'll be making lame excuses. Worrying about money on holiday is the biggest turn off in the world. If you fret about cash, give yourselves a break during your holiday. That doesn't mean maxing out your credit card and coming home planning what you are going to give the debt recovery thugs next week.

Be happy with what you've got. If you're going on a beach holiday you are going to see lots of gorgeous women with fantastic bodies – better than hers. She'll be hiding her orange peel legs with a huge sarong while exotic beauties sashay past you on their way to the pool. Have you taken a look in the mirror recently? You can bet there are plenty of sexier men than you, but do you see her comparing?

Persuasion
Techniques

These persuasion techniques can be used in many different areas of your life, but you'll find them especially useful in a romantic relationship.

••

Effective communicators resolve arguments, assert themselves to get what they want and get laid more often than ineffective ones. Whether you want to spice up your sex life (see page 48) or go out with the lads (see page 83), practise these ten tips.

1. Focus on the common ground. If you want her to accept that your way is best, emphasise your shared values.

2. If you want her to see your point of view, sell it to her with enthusiasm. It is difficult to ignore a person who has the power of their convictions. 'Darling, I've had a really exciting idea . . .'

3. Compare what you want with what has been achieved successfully by another couple. For example, 'Stuart and Jenny have experimented with S&M and say it has deepened their relationship . . .'

4. Be persistent but don't give her an ultimatum or back her into a corner. A drip, drip method is much more effective. Begin with, 'Do you think we could possibly . . .'. If a request is too forceful she will dig her heels in and say no. If you want to buy a new hi-fi system and she wants new carpets, keep the pressure up by reminding her. Cut clippings out of magazines and stick them on the fridge; mention it in passing several times a day.

5. Get her to agree to a trial run. 'If we don't like it, we can always take it back to the shop . . .'

6. If you want her to change her behaviour, be affectionate and caring while giving her constructive criticism.

7. Ask for support: 'What would it take for you to see my point of view?'

8. Bribe your friends and family to back you up. The more people she sees that share your view, the weaker her argument becomes.

9. Persuasive people get what they desire by helping others achieve their goals. Don't just focus on yourself. Understand what she needs from a situation or reach a compromise where both of you feel like you are getting a result.

10. Thanking her in advance is a great way of making her do something. For example, 'I can't wait to see what you've bought me for my birthday. You're so thoughtful, I just know it will be something really special . . .' Do you think she'll buy you something lame after a build up like that?

How to Tell if You're in Love

The most important factor governing your discovery of true love is how you define 'love'. Many people throw away perfectly good relationships because they have an unrealistic or idealised notion of it.

....

1. Your friends' opinions don't seem as important – you don't care that they can't see what you see. If you don't love someone you're always looking for the approval of others, but when you're in love you don't have to justify the great feeling to anyone. You don't care why it's happened – just that it has.

2. You have an incredible amount of energy; you can focus on things that normally would have your mind wandering within a few minutes. You feel more creative. You'll squeeze in another hour of productive work because you know that you'll be meeting her this evening.

3. Your self-esteem is sky high. You feel calm and fulfilled. You don't notice other women – sure, you can find another woman attractive, but you are free from that gnawing desire to find someone special. You know you've already found her.

4. You don't mind what you do with her so long as you are together – sitting next to her watching a lame chick flick is amazing because you feel an incredible electricity coming off her just because she is inches away. Sparks could jump between you and you fear they may set your sofa alight.

5. You don't want to spend time apart and when you do you're always thinking of her.

6. Whatever she wears you think she looks fantastic. You don't spend time wanting her to change bits of herself. You're interested in the whole package and wouldn't change a thing. In fact you don't want her to change at all. She gets a haircut and it upsets you because you thought it was perfect already.

7. You're planning a future with her – spending the rest of your life together doesn't seem the big deal that it did with previous girlfriends.

OK that's a good start but you think that is love? It sounds a bit one-sided – all about what you're feeling and what you are getting from the relationship. If you feel all that during the first few months of a relationship it's a great sign, but love is much more.

Love hangs around even when the initial intensity of feeling has cooled down. And it will cool down. When you're in the first throes of love there is a chemical that is released into your brain called phenylethylamine and it functions much like an amphetamine. That's why you feel so high. But you can't stay high forever. You develop a tolerance.

Neurobiologists reckon it takes about four years for the chemical to fade. Ergo – everlasting love must be more than a load of chemicals.

Life kind of gets in the way. Six things that cause conflict in relationships: money, sex, in-laws, child rearing, roles and religion. As the months pass you'll learn more about each other. Her habits will begin to irritate you. You'll find yourself having to compromise certain areas of your life to keep her happy. You might even start to feel bored.

Does that mean you're not in love? Not if you have a realistic and giving attitude. At this stage the takers quit, but the givers recognise that hard times are an inevitable part of a loving relationship. If you think that's just the talk of someone who has 'settled' then you have an unrealistic expectation about love. When you are always looking for the permanent high, you will never discover true love that comes from commitment – taking the highs with the lows. Many relationships fall down because one party courts nostalgia, 'Why can't it be like it was in the beginning?'

This isn't settling down. It's growing up and realising that love is a more complicated and wonderful thing than the two-dimension fantasy we carry in our heads and see on the movie screen. You can't compare your 'love' to an ideal. It doesn't just come from the heart – it's a mixture of head and heart. It's not something that happens to you – it's a process in which you must be an active participant.

So how to tell if you're in love? Ask yourself whether you are mature and capable enough of understanding and expressing it.

GETTING ON WITH HER PARENTS

One minute you're going steady with a beautiful woman you adore, then you meet her parents. Her mum looks like a mountain goat, and you think 'that's got to be her stepmother. Is that what my honey is going to look like in thirty years time?'

....

Then her father steps out of the shadows, grips your hand in a bonecrusher and you think, 'Oh my god – it's her, without the long hair and soft skin. I'm dating her dad.'

OK, that's the worst case scenario. But if it does happen, under no circumstances should you take refuge in the under-stairs cupboard. Look like son-in-law material and focus on making the right first impression. Even if you are the most eligible bachelor in the world, when you meet her parents for the first time they will be picturing their grandchildren with your nose and generally scrutinising you to see whether you are good enough for their precious daughter.

Put on your best 'I respect your daughter' act. There is no getting away from the unspoken fact that you're shagging her. They don't need reminding. This means no necking on the sofa when their backs are turned. They want to know that you are treating her well too. Don't be tempted to get physical in order to demonstrate how much you're into her. Even stroking hair and cuddling says, 'Push off. Family time is over. Now she's my sex toy.'

Be nice and polite and show you really care about their daughter – in a Platonic way. If she is as serious about you as she has told them, they may have to fork out for a wedding, so they want to know that you're worth it (or they may pay you lip service because you're the fifth man she's brought home in as many months). They want to know you won't pollute their family line with loser genes.

Three parent types to look out for:
Daddy's girl: You've stolen his daughter and her cherry (it wasn't you, but he doesn't know that). He's also jealous of you because it reminds him how much fun he had when he was your age. He will shake your hand harder than you shake his.

Mum's a flirt: She's the mum who comes on. Despite having many chins, you don't know which one she's going to talk out of next and she'll flutter her eyelashes as you help her with the washing-up. She figures if you fancy her daughter there's a chance you might feel the same about her.

Welcome to the family: After half an hour they claim you're like the son the never had. They know so much about you it makes you suspect they've hired a private detective. They tell you to make yourself at home, then exchange knowing glances when you reach into the fridge to make yourself a sandwich. When you break up, they'll send you dead animals and hate mail.

THE POWER
OF FLATTERY

Flattery has been described as the infantry of negotiation. Everyone likes it, and with women you should lay it on with a trowel. Several times a day, every day. And you can't just flatter her once – you've got to repeat it. It's no good saying, 'Of course you have beautiful eyes. I told you last week, remember?'

....

Don't compliment a woman on something that is clearly her best feature. For example, if she has fantastic breasts then don't point them out. Even if you're really only interested in feeling the weight of them against your own naked chest (she knows you like them – you've buried your head between them so many times she's lost count). Complimenting her on something she doesn't feel secure about, like her dainty little feet (she thinks they're too big) will have toe-curling impact. Even an insult can become a compliment if you choose your words carefully. (Telling her you love her aquiline nose sounds romantic, even though you really mean it looks like an eagle's beak.)

If she has had a haircut or is wearing a new item of

clothing, point this out. If you don't, not only will you lose the opportunity of a compliment, but also you'll irritate her through your lack of awareness.

For even greater impact, compliment her on personality and behaviour. She will love to hear that she moves gracefully or she has a sensitive voice. This is more imaginative than copping a feel and telling her she has tight buns. She wants to feel cherished, not ogled. Praise her great sense of humour, or her people skills, or tell her she's a really good listener. Women are sociable animals, so acknowledging that her social skills are top notch will really hit the spot.

Listening is the sincerest form of flattery. Pay attention to what she is thinking and feeling and show genuine interest in her day by asking questions and actually listening to her replies. Let her believe that she is teaching you something new every day. Actually, if you can't learn something new about your partner every day, then what's the point?

Finally, don't let her change you into something you aren't, but do try to be the sort of person that she wants to be with. It's the best form of flattery because it demonstrates that you respect her opinions and that she matters to you.

ohhhh,
you're such a great
listener.

Ten Ideas for Jazzing up Your Sex Life

Living with one woman doesn't have to be dull and boring. Sure, life gets in the way, but there are plenty of simple things you can do to put zest back into your sex.

....

Less is More
Sometimes it pays to get back to basics and concentrate on one activity at a time rather than going for the whole smorgasbord in one session. Try kissing and cuddling without sex or bringing each other to orgasm without intercourse. Restricting your options can be just as exciting as pushing back the boundaries.

Going Commando
Take her out for a romantic date and ask her to leave her underwear in the top drawer. Your shared secret should add an erotic thrill to the evening. Being a little bit naughty in an innocent way will heighten anticipation of things to come.

Have an Affair
With each other. Book yourselves into a hotel using a false name.

Be vocal

Always show your partner how turned on you are during sex. If you love to hear her squeal with delight, you can bet she feels the same way.

Take Me

Take it in turns to be at each other's mercy. You don't have to tie each other up and spank each other to play around with sub-domination themes. There's nothing more thrilling than giving yourself over to your trusted partner and telling her she can do whatever she like with you.

What's Your Name?

Pretend you've just met. Chat each other up in a prearranged location – a bar or restaurant. Arrive separately and spend some time eyeing each other up. Get talking and flirting – see where it takes you. That's a chat up with a hundred per cent chance of success.

Running Commentary

Talk about what you intend to do to each other and keep up a running commentary while you do it. It can lend an intriguing and steamy detachment to a session that can make you feel like you're a voyeur or taking part in a steamy movie.

Shag Week

Nominate a week where you have to have sex at least twice a day for a whole week. You can add extra rules like you can't use the same position twice, or you can't have sex in the same place or room more than once. By the end of the week, you'll be doing it in the airing cupboard.

Forfeits

Play a board game where you have to give each

Wanna play doctors and nurses?

other sexy forfeits. For instance, you can play Monopoly and let her off the fine for landing on Mayfair if she'll give you a blow job.

SCRUB UP

Remember in the early days of your relationship, how much time you took to make yourself look and smell nice for her before a hot date? If you both spend time making yourself irresistible and try to maintain those standards, you'll both feel much more like jumping into the sack at a moment's notice.

DEALING WITH HER JEALOUSY

If your girlfriend gets jealous when you talk to other women, recognise that it means she is interested in you.

....

Be honest and ask yourself whether she has any real cause for concern. Do you enjoy flirting with other women? Do you ignore her at parties so you can talk to other women? Are you uncomfortable showing affection to her in public? Have you ever cheated on her? If so, is it any wonder that she feels so insecure?

If you can say 'yes' to any of the above, it's down to you to make a change to your behaviour. If you really care about her then this should be easy. There's no such thing as harmless flirting. If you're confident about yourself and your relationship, you shouldn't need to flirt, no matter how 'innocent'.

It may be that no matter how much you reassure her that she is the only one for you, she still lacks trust. Maybe she has been badly let down in the past and needs reassurance that you won't treat her the same way. Give her time and keep showing her that she has nothing to worry about. If you're trustworthy, eventually you'll earn her trust.

It's great to reach a place in a relationship where you can both appreciate that you will find others attractive without it meaning that you will run off with the first person that catches your eye. Just because you are hooked up with someone doesn't mean that you won't find others attractive. However, you can control what you do with those feelings. Crushes don't develop out of thin air. They are allowed room to grow. It's all a matter of choice. What do you want most, your girlfriend, or someone else? Do you want to destroy what you have for the sake of a quick fling?

If she really is a lost cause, then her demands on you will become more and more oppressive and unreasonable. If you find that you can't even talk to another woman without having a huge row with your girlfriend afterwards, then it may be time to call it a day.

Going Out with the Lads Whenever You Want

Let's examine the reasons why she should be unhappy or reluctant to let you go out with the lads without putting up a fight, or whinging about how you never spend enough time cuddling her on the sofa.

....

1. She thinks that you will be having a better time without her than with her

Underplay the event. Don't make a big deal about what a great night you are going to have. Make it look like you are a reluctant participant but not too much or she'll make you promise to come home early. When you leave give her a big hug and tell her you'll miss her.

Give her something to do while you're out. This can be anything from renting a girlie movie to encouraging her to have some girlfriends round – that way she can get to complain about you to her friends and she won't feel alone and abandoned.

2. She believes you will act inappropriately

Women hate it when we come home so drunk that we fall over six times on our way to the bedroom then twist an ankle while undressing. You may have felt reasonably sober until you those four chasers at midnight, but if you demonstrate gross lack of control at this stage she will rightly assume you've enjoyed a wild and excessive evening.

3. SHE'LL GET WOKEN UP
Women will always go to bed earlier than normal when you go out, so that they can pretend they were so lonely while you were away. They can also criticise you for waking them up from a deep sleep when you come in. Make sure you end up in bed – don't collapse on the sofa – again that demonstrates incapacity. Stay sober enough that you can get into bed without waking her up.

4. SHE THINKS YOU WILL BREAK PROMISES
Don't try to lessen the impact of a night on the tiles by making promises you do not intend to keep, like 'I won't come back drunk' or 'I'll only have three drinks' or 'I won't do anything stupid'.

Give her a realistic time when you will be home and stick to it. She'll feel more betrayed if you tell her you'll be back at 11.00pm and then come home at 12.00 than if you told her 2.00am and come home an hour early. That way, you get to stay out as long as you want, but she still feels like she has control over you.

Avoid making one specific night sacrosanct. Then if you want to go out twice in one week she'll think you've broken some sort of one-a-week thing. Instead, make a rule that gives you plenty of flexibility and stick to it, like 'I'll never go out more than four times in a row'. She will be happy that you have set 'limits' even though you'll never reach them.

How to Argue

No one can win an argument because by definition it is a fight between two people who don't want to agree. If there was the possibility of an agreement, it would be a discussion.

....

You can't win an argument with a woman. The best a man can hope for is a stalemate.

Women know this. That's why men and women argue differently. A man argues to win, while a woman argues to make a man lose. Instead of focusing on herself, or logic, her energy is directed towards making him commit an unforced error.

It's like playing tennis. She wins by keeping the ball in play until you make a mistake. That's why she'll bring up all sorts of irrelevancies and go off at a tangent. She won't listen to reason and gets more and more worked up. It doesn't matter how skilfully

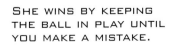

SHE WINS BY KEEPING
THE BALL IN PLAY UNTIL
YOU MAKE A MISTAKE.

85

you hit the ball because actually you're not playing tennis at all – you're knocking up against a wall and she's the wall. The wall never loses. It just keeps returning the ball until you eventually cock it up.

When a man and woman argue, he's trying not to lose his temper and she's trying not to cry. The trouble is, if either of these things happen, she wins. She keeps the barriers up until either of these things happen. If you lose your temper, she can score double points by bursting into tears.

You often hear the advice, 'stick to the point' – that's fine, but don't expect it to work. Don't expect logic to work either.

Whatever happens, don't lose your temper and don't make her cry – she can do that all by herself, and she will – it's just a matter of time. Once she realises that you are staying calm she will employ her only remaining option: spontaneous weeping. Watch carefully for the moment when it looks like she is about to blub then start crying too and give her a hug. You can both hug each other and have a good sob then kiss and make up. Stalemate. At least you haven't had to apologise.

How to Get Her to Share Your Interest in Pornography

Pornography has always been a very controversial subject and it has existed since the first caveman drew a picture of a naked bison being fisted on the wall of his cave. The word 'pornography' comes from the ancient Greek *porne* and *graphos*, meaning 'writing about prostitutes'.

....

The Romans used explicit erotic scenes as part of their everyday internal decoration – you have to admit that their fantasies were pretty much out in the open. Having your own interests is healthy, but having a secret stash is just not a good thing. Give it up, or share – your fantasies, that is.

OK, you're probably thinking, 'What, are you crazy?' You don't want to tell her about your secret room. You know. The one where you twist a coat hook three inches to the right and the whole wall swings back to reveal a porno den that can rival Hugh Hefner's.

Don't you think it's kind of sad? Without getting into the rights and wrongs of porn, what sort of relationship have you got if there's a whole side to your sex life that you are both missing out on?

Actually, it's kind of hard to imagine Cro-Magnon Man beating himself off to some illicit cave drawings. Wouldn't he have expressed his sexuality more directly than us? It's ironic that the repressed Victorians have undoubtedly contributed to today's global porn industry. It thrives because couples aren't communicating their sexual preferences or have inhibitions they're unwilling to share.

Undoubtedly, some women enjoy using porn, but the problem is that most of it is geared towards men rather than couples. Only ten per cent of men use porn to benefit the couple. Many women find the idea of pornography degrading and disgusting. If your partner is one of these then you should question your use of pornography at all. But at the end of the day, it's about fantasy – so why not involve her in yours? Most male fantasies are relatively tame, but it's all too easy to point your mouse at some naughty nurses rather than tell her you would love to see her in a uniform.

Being honest about what turns you on will benefit the two of you much more than pleasuring yourself in private.

Giggle...

KEEPING YOUR COOL

**Anger is a natural emotion. You can't
prevent it but you can harness it. It's
one thing to know in your mind that
anger doesn't solve problems, but it's
another to actually believe it and put
it into practice.**

....

In a relationship, anger usually erupts where there
has been a break down in communication and it is
nearly always related to the frustration of unmet
expectations. How often do you hear children angrily
saying, 'But, it's not fair . . .' We expect one thing
and get another, or else we confuse a desire with
a demand, thinking we have a right for something
to happen a certain way just because we desire it.

If you can learn to see anger as a failure rather
than as a call to action, if you absolutely refuse
to allow yourself the option of being angry, you'll
be amazed at the alternative strategies you will
develop to solve your problems. But don't think in
terms of bottling up your anger. Think instead of
'conserving' your anger so that you can direct this
energy into constructive action.

For example, in Sweden it is illegal for parents to
smack their children, and as a result, Swedish
parents are often incredibly adept at negotiating

with their kids to resolve disputes or behaviour difficulties without getting angry and lashing out. Take away anger and violence as an option and you are forced to use more productive solutions.

Communicate your problems in order to find a resolution. This means describing the problem to your partner and expressing in an assertive, non-aggressive way how it makes you feel. Beware of hyperbole! Being angry makes your thoughts exaggerated: 'You always . . . you never . . . I've told you a thousand times . . . I hate you . . . I never loved you . . .' Beware also of expressing your anger indirectly in 'passive-aggressive' behaviour – sulking, being sarcastic, refusing to talk.

There's an old Buddhist story about an angry young man who went to his teacher for advice about how to control his temper. The teacher said, 'Show me this anger, it sounds fascinating.' But the man replied, 'I can't show it to you now, I don't have it.' So the teacher suggested, 'Well, bring it to me when you are angry' to which the young man replied, 'I wouldn't be able to keep it long enough to bring to you. By the time I had walked to your house, I would no longer be angry.' The teacher smiled and said, 'In that case, next time you are angry, close your eyes and pretend you are walking to my house.'

#

COMMUNI-
CATE YOUR
PROBLEMS
IN ORDER
TO FIND
A RESOLU-
TION.

LEARNING TO LISTEN

Listening can be a pain in the arse. She's telling you something you've heard before or she's nagging again. You're preoccupied, missing your favourite movie or most likely just want to go to sleep. We men always have a good excuse for not listening, then wonder why we have a reputation as bad listeners.

....

Lack of communication is one of the biggest reasons why relationships fail. Listening is a skill which involves more than giving your own mouth a rest. You actually have to give your thoughts a rest too, because they are the main barriers to effective listening. It's so easy to start analysing or be reminded of something you want to say, then stop listening and wait for your turn to speak.

Stop whatever you are doing and give her your full attention. You may feel perfectly capable of stripping down a motorcycle engine while she pours her heart out, but she'll only storm off meaning you'll have to spend twice as long apologising and then listening. Listening saves time in the long run.

So, you're listening and she's talking about how there was no broccoli at the supermarket, but believe it or not, she's not really talking about broccoli. Whatever the vegetable, she's revealing her feelings. Your job is to validate those feelings. It's that simple. It's much harder to be judgmental ('You should shop somewhere else') or provide reasons ('They always run out of broccoli on Fridays'). She doesn't want an explanation of why the stock levels were inadequate or advice about where she should shop. She doesn't even care about broccoli. She simply wants emotional validation. She just wants you to hear you say something like 'You must have felt very frustrated. You're working so hard, I bet you're exhausted.'

Never say 'don't worry' – that's like saying what she feels doesn't matter, even if you are trying to help. If you're not sure what she is telling you, ask questions until you have homed in on her feelings. She may be really excited about something that you find so boring or uninteresting it makes you want to chew your arm off. Again, search for her excitement and share it. If she wants you to participate in her delight, what's wrong with that?

You want to be noticed too – what about what you have to say? Well, be assured that she will notice you more when you are actively listening than at any other time. Good listening leads to emotional intimacy, which leads straight to the bedroom. So it's worth learning how to do it and that doesn't just mean raising your eyebrows and staring at her lips wondering when she's going to shut up.

Learning Not
to Say 'Sorry'

**What's happened to us? We've become so
hung up on compensating for the fact
that women have been given a raw deal
for thousands of years that we can't
stop apologising and making up for the
shortcomings of the male race.**

....

If you cave in at every little demand, in the end she
will lose all respect for you and go and find a man
who treats her mean and keeps her keen. Sure, if
you've been unfaithful or forgotten her birthday,
say you're sorry and move on. However, there are
lots of occasions when you shouldn't grovel.

1. Not shaving
Doesn't she realise that shaving strips away layers
of skin and makes your face dry and sore? She
should be thankful you have a job where a little
stubble is a sign of creativity and originality. She
spends hundreds on skin care products, so why
shouldn't you look after your skin too and actually
save money?

2. Not being telepathic
How can you know what's on her mind if she
doesn't tell you?

Don't apologise for anything involving sports, cars, gadgets, being obsessive, crotch scratching, technology or booze.

3. STAYING LATE AT WORK

Either you get a low-paid job so that you can be home in time for dinner, or you put in the hours and give her all the material comforts she demands. She can't have it both ways.

4. NOT SHARING HER LAME TASTE IN TV PROGRAMMES

If you can't bear to be in the room while she's watching her favourite soap opera, don't apologise for snowboarding on your Xbox instead. She can't expect you to keep her company on the sofa when she's watching crap TV.

5. TELLING HER MOTHER TO BUTT OUT
Her mother may be able to interfere in her daughter's life, but you shouldn't have any worries about telling her when she's crossed the line with you. A little look here and 'innocent' remark there works wonders. You don't want to be bullied by two women do you?

6. LEAVING THE TOILET SEAT UP
She should stand when she's peeing, then the toilet seat can stay up all the time (see page 24).

7. SKIPPING THE FOREPLAY, SOMETIMES
It's OK for her to jump on you when she's feeling horny. Do you ever hear a man complain about needing to get in the mood?

8. COMING HOME DRUNK
Why does she feel so insulted when you stagger home rat-arsed? So what if you fall over while taking your trousers off; that's supposed to happen when you're drunk. At least you haven't developed a tolerance to alcohol. Then she should really be worried.

9. DOING MANLY THINGS
Don't apologise for anything involving sports, cars, gadgets, being obsessive, crotch scratching, technology or booze.

10. NOT WANTING KIDS YET
If men didn't put the reins on breeding, the planet would be uninhabitable already. It's up to you to get her to be realistic about what having a baby entails.

TELLING WHITE LIES

When you were a child you spoke like a child, thought like a child and lied like a child. In fact there were lots of things you stunk at, like picking up hamsters without squeezing them to death, or drinking coffee or not peeing in the swimming pool but did you stop doing any of these things? No, you kept on practising until you got better.

. . . .

It's the same with lying. As a boy you learned that lying was wrong because you always got caught out. Instead you should have figured that kids just can't lie very well.

Now you're an adult you've left your childish ways behind you (yeah, right!). You recognise that life isn't black and white, that moral boundaries are blurred. A relationship without honesty is doomed, but too much of a good thing is always bad. There are times when a harmless lie can make the difference between making your partner feel like a goddess or a witch.

NO, YOU DON'T NEED TO LOSE WEIGHT
No, she doesn't need to. She could use a little streamlining, but unless she's clinically obese, don't

allow even a hint of thinking time when she asks if she's fat. 'Needs to' is when she's so huge she can't fetch you another beer from the kitchen without getting breathless.

I LOVE YOU JUST THE WAY YOU ARE
Billy Joel sure can lie! Is it any wonder his song was such a smash hit? Women can't get enough of this one and you can use it to answer almost any difficult questions she throws at you from 'should I change my hair colour' to 'should I buy a new outfit?'

YES, I LOVE YOUR COOKING
So what if she can't make roast potatoes like your mum or her cooking is so bad even the dog goes next door to eat. Let her feel like she's a home-maker and maybe she'll keep faking her orgasms.

OF COURSE I DON'T FANCY HER
Yeah you do, but she doesn't need the complicated answer that you look but don't touch. Just keep things simple and remember that you only have eyes for her.

I'M SORRY
And you've come full circle. Remember what you used to say to your mum all those years ago when she discovered you'd been lying?

Buying Her Lingerie

Guys are visual. We can't help it. We get excited with what we see in front of us or in our imaginations, especially a when it's a beautiful woman in sexy lingerie. So, when you're undressing her you don't want so see that washed-out two-set that makes her look more like your granny than a sex kitten.

....

Treat her to some new lingerie and it's a win-win situation so long as you know what to choose to make her feel special. Get it right and she will feel feminine and sexy and you're halfway to getting some action. Get it wrong and she'll feel like a cheap slut, or worse, that you're dissatisfied with her.

So, what makes the difference between classy hot stuff and cheap sleaze?

First, choose something that she is comfortable wearing. That means styles that suit her body and her personality. Choose lingerie that draws attention to her best features (that's the ones she likes, which may be different to your favourites! You may love her nipples but that doesn't give you carte blanche to buy her a Peek-A-Boo bra with tassels.) Think looker rather than hooker and go for coverage over skimpy.

Women are touch oriented. Feel the material: if it's soft and silky she'll feel comfortable wearing it. Lace looks pretty but it can feel like sack cloth against the skin.

Drop some huge coin. Choose something she wouldn't buy herself that she would love to receive.

If you want to see her in something different, take small steps – don't buy her latex crotchless panties if you know she'll freak and throw them back in your face. If she normally wears granny pants, then ease her in gently. Buy her something a little different, but close to what she already wears and feels happy with.

Check out her existing bra and panties for sizes. On bras, the letters (A, B, C, D etc.) refer to the size of the breast while the number (32, 34, 36, 38) is the measurement around her back.

Alternatively, decide which piece of fruit best describes her breasts. For a rough cup size: Lemons=A; Orange=B; Grapefruit=C and Melons=D.

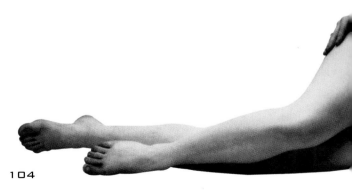

Be confident and casual when you're in the shop. Not everyone is going to think you're either a perv or a tranny.

Put them in a box and wrap them up – don't just thrust a carrier bag towards her and grunt 'put them on' while unzipping your flies. You can even put a card, chocolates, jewellery or perfume in the box too for extra romantic effect.

It's a thrill to know that she will soon be peeling them off for an exclusive audience of one – you. No matter what, tell her she looks sexy – now is not the time to point out her inadequacies. Build her confidence now and she'll become a nubile nymph eager to satisfy your every desire.

Lemons = A
Orange = B
Grapefruit = C
Melons = D

I'm definitely a lemon!

Coping with Her Mood Swings

If men are supposed to be experts at bottling up their emotions, then women have turned unpredictability into an art form. One minute you're the golden boy who can do no wrong, the next you're a layabout who walks all over her taking her for granted.

....

From the killer hormones of PMS to the hot flushes of menopause, women spend thirty years of their life reverting to adolescence every few weeks.

But it's hard to sympathise when they believe it's their prerogative to let their emotions run out of control, then criticise us for pointing it out. God help us if we suggest that they've got PMS or mid-cycle blues. They say it's because they are more in touch with their emotions than men. We're in touch, but we just have more minimalist methods when it comes to expressing them.

Wait a minute: don't women criticise us for being predictable – that's what we do best, isn't it? We're consistently boorish, sport loving, insensitive and take them for granted all the time, aren't we?

So it must be her reaction that changes. This is the same breed that endures toe-shortening and nail-narrowing surgery to fit into pointy-toed shoes and undergoes boob jobs and tummy tucks. They've grown up watching icons like Madonna and Kylie Minogue changing their image every three weeks. Unpredictability is an integral part of the media's representation of sexuality. For the woman in the street who can't swim with the big fishettes who create a sexual mystique by continually changing their physical appearance, a bipolar personality is the next obvious choice.

There's nothing you can do about it. It is PMS even though she won't admit it, and the rest of the time it's post or pre PMS. Just don't let her fool you into thinking otherwise or even bite your head off for suggesting what we all know – that she is ruled by her hormones, just like we're ruled by our peckers.

Amanda showed her frustration as Man Utd went 2-1 up.

DEALING WITH HER MIND GAMES

Somebody once said that taking cocaine is like dropping an atomic bomb on your brain. It's the same with women. They're a confusing species.

....

You can't win an argument with them, it's certainly not a good idea to pick a fight with them, you have to make them endless cups of tea and continuously feed them chocolate. They want to talk when you're asleep and wake you up to tell you you're snoring. They analyse everything. Women's mind games always boil down to two words: 'guilt trip'. First comes the guilt followed by the trip.

SCENARIO ONE
Her: Are you asleep?
Him: Not any more.
Her: I can't sleep. Your snoring is keeping
me awake.
Him: Oh. Sorry. (Guilt)
Her: Can you fetch me a glass of water?
(Trip: to the kitchen)

SCENARIO TWO
Her: Can we go shopping?
Him: Do we have to?
Her: We don't have to spend any money.
It would be nice to do something together.

IT'S CODE
FOR
'FETCH
YOUR
COAT,
WE'RE
GOING
OUT.'

Him: We're together now, aren't we?

Her: You must really hate me.

Him: No, I don't. (Guilt)

Her: Yes, you do – you never want to spend any time with me.

Him: But I love you.

Her: Then come shopping with me.

(Trip: to the mall)

SCENARIO THREE

Him: What's wrong?

Her: Nothing.

Him: You don't look very happy.

Her: I'm fine, really.
Anyway, you wouldn't understand.

Him: Yes I would. (Guilt)

Her: Can you make me a cup of tea?

(Trip: to the kitchen again)

SCENARIO FOUR

Him: What do you want to do tonight?

Her: I don't mind. You choose.

Him: OK, let's go and see *Kill Bill*.

Her: No, I don't want to go to the cinema.

Him: OK, how about a restaurant? Chinese?

Her: No, I'm not hungry.

Him: Well, there's a good film on TV.

Her: No, I want to do something.

Him: Well, what do you want to do? (Guilt)

Her: I don't mind. You choose.

(Trip: to the movies, eventually, to see another mawkish mother-daughter saga with no real plot about a bunch of Louisiana ladies cooking and talking a lot to try to understand their painful past)

There's nothing you can do. Just understand that if an argument ends with the complaint that she isn't getting enough romantic attention, it's code for 'fetch your coat, we're going out.'

GREAT SEX IN THE SHOWER

Just when you think the sex can't get any better, she disappears into the bathroom and you hear the sound of running water. She builds up a roomful of steam then appears in the doorway naked holding a large loofah and beckons you into her watery den. She wants to know if you can make her sing in the shower. Well can you?

Wait! Don't jump into the shower together. Why not let her go in first and start washing. Stand watching her for a while, catching glimpses of her gorgeous body between gaps in the shower curtain. It will increase the anticipation for both of you until the moment you step in to join her.

Now spend a few minutes washing and teasing each other sensually. It's wonderfully intimate and makes you feel privileged to be invited into her world. Start with her back and work your way down to her buttocks and thighs. If it starts off innocently, it will be much more of a thrill when it becomes sexual – and it will – very quickly. There's something about making out in the shower that makes you want to get on with it – it's a combination of the warmth and the urgent rush of water that cranks up the pace.

Use the showerhead to pleasure her downstairs. Don't be too caught up on penetrative sex – it looks easy in the movies, but mutual masturbation can give you much more flexibility and pleasure in a confined space.

The warm water will be helping the blood flow in your penis and her vagina – it's aquatic Viagra. Are you having fun yet? Oh what the hell – lift her up, bend her over and send your U-boat into her harbour. Make sure there's no soap on you before you penetrate her – she won't appreciate it and it's not a good lubricant.

A hot shower doesn't kill sperm.

If you're going to attempt stand up sex (like in the movies) – this is much harder than it looks. It requires co-ordination, strength and rubber suckers on your feet to stop you from slipping over. For deeper penetration she should stand on one leg and hook the other one around yours, while you support her thigh with your hand. Then you can rock her back and forth. Only pick her up completely if she's much lighter than you are!

It's a myth that having sex in a hot shower kills sperm so she can't get pregnant. That's an old wives' tale and what do they know about steamy shower sex?

Taking a Break

There are times when a relationship reaches breaking point; where one or both of you feel you need your own space and time apart from the other in the hope that this will benefit the relationship in the long run. But does taking a break signal the beginning of the end or can it really be a good way to test the strength of feeling between you and resolve important issues?

....

If you decide to take a break you need to lay down some important parameters. Be clear how long you agree to separate before coming back together to discuss your future. Also be clear whether you must still be exclusive or are both free to date other people during this period. This is especially important since poor communication is already likely to be an issue.

Time alone will not of itself solve major problems in a relationship; once you get back together they will still be there. The benefit of a separation is that it allows both of you the space to work on the issues that you have both agreed are an obstacle to your future together. It also gives you a healthy distance from which to gain a more realistic perspective.

If only one partner feels the need to take a break, it can feel like a betrayal for the other, but the fact that it has reached this point will mean that the relationship will break up soon if no constructive action is taken. Sometimes, the person who didn't want the break discovers that they didn't like the person they had become within the relationship, and it may be them that breaks it off, after reaching an objective decision that simply would have been impossible within the confines of 24/7 togetherness.

We all form various habits and patterns within a relationship, some good, some bad. Spending time apart can be a revelation in helping recognise them. Sometimes just the separation itself is enough to break the cycle of destructive behaviour.

So it's wrong to think of a separation as a wholly negative thing if you both use the time to rediscover your individuality, the positive feelings that you have for each other and the negative aspects of your own personality that need changing. When you get back together you will know how to work to become an even stronger unit.

Relationships are risky. Falling in love is risky. Making a commitment to spend the rest of your life with someone is mind-blowing. Try to see taking a break as just another one of those risks.

How to Enjoy Shopping

Why do we hate shopping so much and what can we do to minimise our angst when dragged to the mall by our partners?

. . . .

Some feminists would have you believe that to hate shopping is to hate women, that anti-consumerism is misogyny because it's the one arena where they truly exercise choice and can reinvent themselves (plastic surgery being the pinnacle of consumption). But let's face it: they only need us there to park the car, carry their bags and lie to them about the size of their backside.

Is it because malls remind us just how much like everyone else we are? Men can see this because we are the architects of globalisation. Not us, personally of course, but the handful of moguls who drive the world economy. Shopping is a threat to a man's sense of individuality. We hate the possibility that we might be manipulated into making the likes of Bill Gates even richer.

Or is it that we're just useless browsers? The hunter-gatherer would go out with the express intention of killing an animal and dragging it home. He didn't say 'Oh, I'll just tramp around the savannah for a while and see what takes my fancy.

Look, Roger – isn't that llama just to die for?'
Men had to make instant decisions and bring back
a kill. They didn't return from a hunt saying,
'I couldn't find a wildebeest in a size twelve.'
Equivocation equalled starvation. Consequently,
men hate being in a state of indecision. It's
inefficient and unmanly.

But the real reason why shopping with women is
horrible is because she makes all the decisions,
whether she's shopping for herself or forcing you to
buy a new shirt. No wonder she feels so empowered.

There is really only one way in which you can
reclaim control. Join the struggle against
consumerism. Do it now, after all, it does destroy
the environment and your bank balance. You can
do this either in a large way, by quitting your job
and growing your own vegetables, or by behaving
absurdly while shopping (small-scale retail
disobedience – SRD).

Seven Acts of SRD

1 **Try on every tie in the shop and leave
without buying anything.**

2 **Drink ten Starbuck's mocha lattes in a
row then pretend you're Tyler Durden in
Fight Club.**

3 Act suspiciously. Do not steal anything, but look really shifty. If a store detective stops you (which they're not allowed to do, because they won't have actually seen you stealing anything), you may get a free gift voucher when they realise they've made an embarrassing mistake.

4 In homage to Ozu Yasujiro's classic film *Ohayo*, refuse to talk until she buys you something with a plug on it.

5 When food shopping, unwrap all your purchases at the checkout and ask to see their company policy on waste management regulations.

6 Scream every eight seconds to express the pain of deforestation.

7 Pretend you've lost a fictitious child.

How to Be Worshipped
in the Bedroom

**Who do you think has the bigger pecker –
an Argentine lake duck or a 460-pound
adult male gorilla? (We're not talking
beaks, here.) It isn't a trick question,
although the answer is surprising.**

....

Not only is the duck's tackle longer – it's three
times longer. Respect to the duck. In fact, a
gorilla's erection is a mere two inches in length.
(Not that remarkable when you consider that he
faces less competitive sexual access than a duck
or a human. He only needs to get laid a few times
each year and has a harem of up to six lady
gorillas. So – size really doesn't matter.)

What does this teach us? It indicates that as far
as sex is concerned, you can't take anything for
granted (and that eating bananas may make your
jigger shrink). Sex is more wonderfully complex
and intricate than we can imagine and has endless
possibilities. If you bring this attitude into the
bedroom you won't go far wrong.

Mix it up
There is no definite way of having great sex. Sir
Laurence Olivier once came off stage in a blind

rage after giving one of the best performances of his life. He was angry because he didn't know how he had done it or how to recreate it. It's the same with making love. You can't plan earth-shattering sex, you just have to be willing to explore, be spontaneous and leave yourself open to those sporadic moments of greatness.

WORSHIP HER OUTSIDE THE BEDROOM
Instead of giving her gifts, treat her as a gift. Make her the focus of your attention, listen to her needs and respect her feelings. Share her interests and do all that romantic stuff you see people doing in films – holding hands on beaches with your trousers rolled up to your knees, watching sunsets, sharing food. Look for the romance in ordinary situations.

TAKE YOUR TIME
Double the amount of time you currently spend on foreplay. Now double it again. Explore her whole body using your whole body.

PAY ATTENTION TO THE DETAILS
The thing that separates genius and beauty from mediocrity and brutishness is attention to detail. It's the difference between creating an intricate mosaic and sticking down lino flooring . Be an intelligent and focused lover. The best sexual technique in the world is attentiveness.

COMMUNICATE
It's great if you can both talk openly about sex and what turns you on but there are other ways to communicate your preferences. Be vocal – give your partner plenty of clues when she is giving you pleasure. Listen and be aware of how her body responds to you. Many men have spent so many of their early years jerking off in clandestine silence

Girls loved Jeff's tight buttocks!

that when it comes to having sex with a woman old habits die hard. Do you orgasm in total silence? Loosen up and express yourself!

ALWAYS PUT HER PLEASURE FIRST
All the best lovers know to put a woman's needs first and that sex begins in the brain.

ASK FOR DIRECTIONS
Sex, like life, is a continual learning process. You draw the map together as you go along. She knows her body better than you, so don't be afraid to stop and ask for directions.

Keeping Her Sweet with Gifts and Flowers

Men don't like giving gifts unless they are practical. With women it's the opposite. The more useless the gift, the greater its impact. A present that has no purpose sends a powerful message: 'I value you so much that I will waste my hard-earned cash on a gift that is totally devoid of function in order to make you happy.' (Don't actually say that.)

....

If you're in a restaurant and one of those hobbling freaks comes in off the street selling 'a single red rose for the laydeeee' then buy it for her and include a handsome tip. She'll be impressed by your extravagant disregard of common sense: 'Look, honey, I'm even prepared to be exploited in public just for you.' The alternative is to spend very little money on something that costs you a large investment of other resources such as your time or health. Let's say she likes ammonites. If you spend three hours on a beach in November trying to find one you will definitely score points, especially if you are bedridden with the flu for the next ten days.

Give a gift from the bottom of your heart, not one that is logical or practical or even expensive. But hang on – isn't love supposed to be non-material? In fairy tales, yes; in real life you will have to buy her stuff and surprise her with it as well. Women like us to be predictable in all areas except the bedroom and the florist.

From the male perspective, flowers would seem to be the epitome of predictability, but to a woman it's wonderful every time she receives them. It's a gift from above – you don't even have to think about it too much, but you do need to remember to remove the half-price sticker if you are buying them from a petrol station after 6.00pm.

Don't feel embarrassed if you're purchasing a cheap arrangement. Many a time the money spent in the florist is more about impressing the usually female shop assistant. They are trained to be discreet and, just like sales assistants in lingerie boutiques, they should be non-judgmental.

You can also buy any gifts that help make her more attractive – make-up, perfume, trips to health spas – anything that makes her feel like she's going to look better afterwards. For some reason this makes them happy rather than making them think you want them to scrub up.

Don't ever give your girl anything that will make the housework easier – you may as well chain her to the vacuum cleaner. She doesn't want to hear the message that you value her as a general skivvy, even if it's true. Make her feel like a goddess. Don't be tempted into buying her that neat gadget you saw on the shopping channel.

As a general rule, the lamer it feels to the man, the more the woman will like it.

WHAT TO DO WHEN SHE WANTS TO HAVE KIDS

Well, there has to be a punishment for having great sex, right? Children are massively selfish and demanding. They break everything, they cost a fortune, they stop you from doing the things you want to do and they generally make huge demands on your relationship.

....

You've always got to put them first, they eat into your time, they're exhausting, they make too much noise, they keep you awake and that's just during the first two years!

Can I have your baby?

Don't let anyone convince you they're worth all the hassle until you're in a position to make up your own mind. Understand the pros and cons of what is involved and decide whether you are prepared to fit your life around your children. Remember, though – life is supposed to be lived and if you're doing it right it's rarely tidy.

Don't ever have kids in order to try to benefit your relationship. Children should be born into a loving and caring household, not one where one party has bowed to pressure from the other, or where both of you are looking for a way to fix something that's broken. Some people have children because they think it will increase the bond between them and their partner – in fact the opposite is true. Having children puts an enormous stress on a relationship and you need an incredibly strong, honest and co-operative partnership to stay together.

Talk to other parents, by all means, but they can't give you the true picture, because they will always punctuate their comments with 'of course, I wouldn't change it for the world'. They may be feeling trapped and miserable (parents of young children do report that they feel less fulfilled than their childless contemporaries) but it will take a lot of coaxing to get them to admit it to themselves, let alone to a third party.

Write down your fears and preconceptions – good and bad – from cost to changing nappies to having teenagers that hate you, your relationship crumbling, the sex ending and her with stress incontinence, jelly briskets and no pelvic floor. Some of your fears will be well founded (although many of those will be self-fulfilling based on your own preconceptions). Many will not. The only thing that is certain about procreation is that some of it will be just like you expected and other bits you can never predict. Whatever picture you have of being a parent – the reality will be very different.

Unfortunately, even getting a puppy is no dry run for starting a family (eventually even puppies stop destroying your property). The only way you can know what having kids is like is by having them. There are no dress rehearsals. The only model you can use is to look back on your own childhood, your relationship with your parents and by talking to your partner. Ensure that the person you are having children with has an incredible capacity to love and nurture that you share, then make a commitment to do everything you can for the livelihood of your new family.

How to Spend More Time with Your PC

Do you remember when you were a kid you spent from the time you got home from school until bedtime squat-thrusting or doing barbell curls to attract the girls? Hours of flip tricks and bench presses and it made absolutely no difference did it? The only guys that got the girls were the ones that were, or had been at some point in their schooling career, captains of the football, rugby and cricket teams.

....

Well now it's time for the rest of us men to get our revenge, because PCs are here to stay and it's one obsession that isn't about impressing the ladies (unless you're some weird blogger who thinks your knowledge of linux systems will get you invited back for coffee). How many hours a day do you squeeze in on your PC? Not enough. When was the last time you switched yours off and had to wave goodbye to your optical two-button scroll wheel mouse? When SHE told you to, most likely.

That's because women hate PCs. They hate the way it appeals to our obsessive-compulsive nature; they hate that it doesn't involve them. So, in order to spend more time with your PC, you've got to convince her that she is still important – not easy when you want to spend Saturday afternoon downloading MP3s and playing Tomb Raider 38, 'Lara Croft and the Curse of the Colostomy Bag'.

Here are ten subtle ways that you can get this message across by making positive associations between her and your PC.

1. Don't call it 'your' PC. Refer to it as 'our' PC and get her to choose a name for it.
2. When she asks you to stop, stop. The quicker you comply with her demand for attention, the less she will need in the long run. If you're about to go out, don't hold her up by checking your emails. The less it interferes with her plans, the more time you can spend with your PC.
3. Use a picture of her as your desktop image and stick another picture on to the monitor. She will think this is cute and love that you are thinking of her.
4. Frequently burn her a smoochy CD of her favourite music.
5. Collect cute JPEGs of her favourite cuddly animals and email them to her.
6. Use the Internet together to search for new restaurants or away-breaks or to book a holiday.
7. Offer to do the grocery shopping then do it online each week.
8. Avoid discussing computer-related stuff with her. This will only fuel her perception that your PC rules your life.
9. While online, send romantic instant messages to her at work.
10. Never sit at the PC in your pyjamas or naked and remember to shave every day.

How to Tell if She's Cheating on You

Trust and intimacy are key to developing strong relationships and cheating damages both, but it can also be a sign that these two ingredients are already missing or being neglected. If you suspect she's cheating on you, the cracks will already be showing.

....

The best way to tell if she's cheating on you is to examine your own behaviour, which should give you all the clues you need. Do you put work before her, do you travel away from home a lot, spend more time watching sport, playing video games, than with her?

It's easy to point the finger at someone else, but if she's cheating, then you have to accept partial responsibility. It's likely that your own behaviour is instrumental in making her stray.

So why do people cheat? It's usually a mixture of two things: physical sexual urges and emotional need. They usually cheat because there is a conflict between what they want physically and emotionally. It's recognised that men aren't monogamous by nature, but neither are women. Monogamy is a trade-off that takes place when certain other conditions are in place; namely stability, emotional connection, physical satisfaction, communication, good parenting and financial security. If there aren't enough of these conditions being met, then there is a decreased incentive for staying faithful. Humans are opportunist by nature and will always look for something better.

So stop treating yourself as a victim or blaming her for being a two-timing cow. If you suspect she's being unfaithful then you need to have an honest consideration of what you are providing for her as an incentive to make her stay faithful to you.

OTHER TELLTALE SIGNS INCLUDE:
1. You're focusing too much on sex and not enough on emotional closeness.
2. You notice a dramatic change in her 'normal' behaviour or routines.
3. She's not as emotionally needy. You treat her badly and she doesn't care as much because she's getting her kicks elsewhere.
4. She's being secretive, discussing her movements less or just being downright evasive.
5. Look out for overcompensating behaviour like being especially nice and buying you gifts.
6. Rely on your gut instincts. They will usually be correct.
7. You communicate poorly at home and spend more time watching TV than talking.
8. Your partner is starting to get more interested in kinky sex, more frequent sex, change in sexual techniques or even less sex.
9. You are unreasonably jealous or untrusting of her and try to control her movements.
10. She's secretive about credit cards slips.

If she's cheating on you take it as a wake-up call that something needs to change in your relationship – that's for both of you.

Moving In – Are You Ready?

You saw your fantastic girlfriend today. How you wish she was here now. You could be shagging on your sofa. You'd be paying less rent and you could wake up to some early morning sex followed by one of her speciality breakfasts. Moving in together seems pretty neat . . . but how can you tell if you're ready?

....

OK, first of all you've got to know what it's really going to be like. Then you can decide whether the new regime will suit you.

Familiarity heralds the loss of a certain mystique. You'll get to see her slobbing around (whenever you've dated she's looked a million dollars). Unfortunately you won't be able to veg out as much as before. She'll probably want the place tidier than you are used to (or vice-versa) – hell, she might even get you to clean the toilet.

Never again will you get to sleep on your own, your wake up time will be dictated by each other's (what if she gets up an hour earlier than you?) and she'll definitely want you to come to bed when she's

You'll have to include each other in your plans, if only to tell her when you're coming home.

ready. No more late-nighters. Make sitting on the toilet special, as it may be the only time you'll get to yourself.

You'll have to include each other in your plans, if only to tell her when you're coming home. She'll be at home with dinner ready or waiting for you to come back and cook for her.

Remember all that bachelor pad furniture? Well, you can bring it into your new love nest, but slowly she'll replace it with a decor that she likes. 'Pink and fluffy' is back in and black leather and chrome are definitely out.

Meals will usually be a compromise (you can't like the same stuff all the time) as will TV viewing – she's got to have her soap opera fix every night. Are you ready for cable warfare?

Is your relationship strong enough to weather the storm of bills and budgeting that goes with running a household? If she spends three times as long on the phone than you, are you happy to split the bill? Plus you'll be making many joint-purchasing decisions – she is more likely to want to spend your money on new curtains than a flat screen TV.

Most importantly – there's no going back. If things don't work out you can't go back to living apart. You will split up.

If you're happy to take the bad with the good, then feather your love nest with essence of girlfriend and find out if she really is 'the one'. The cons are bound to be outweighed by the relentless sex, rental savings and her talents in the kitchen. Plus you get to come home to her every night. Trading freedom for a little more security may be worth it after all. Only time and a lot of compromise will tell.

A piece of advice: Buy the biggest bed you can fit in your bedroom. Take the roof off and lower it in with a crane if you have to. You want a bed with time zones and its own climate. The alternative is sleep deprivation and her elbow in your face every time you turn over.

Are You Ready for Marriage?

Before getting married you should ask yourself far more than twenty questions, but here are some to warm you up:

....

1. Do you love her – really love her, now and forever until she's an old woman with a zimmer frame and moustache? Is your love for her based on what she looks like now, or is it a spark that's inside her, that indefinable something which she will still have even when she's eighty and her breasts swing pendulously at her knees?

2. Do you know her and her opinions well enough? What are her views on marriage, children, money, politics, cheese, religion, adoption, abortion, divorce, family, furniture, curtains, staying late at the office, *The Simpsons*, death, beards . . .?

3. Does she accept you for the man that you are? If you lost your hair, your high-powered job or your marbles, would she still love and cherish you?

4. Are you secretly hoping she'll change something about herself before your wedding day?

5. Do you have roughly the same attitude towards money? Is what's yours, hers?

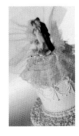

6. Have you had enough sex with other women? Are you ready to accept that you will never get jiggy with anyone but her, ever (unless you're unfaithful or she dies first, but if you've thought of those you're not ready)?

7. From time to time, are you both prepared to turn down an opportunity or experience or accept responsibilities you don't enjoy because it benefits your relationship?

8. Do you trust each other completely?

9. What is most important: what you give or what you get from marriage?

10. Do you respect the notion of 'a marriage' or is it just a piece of paper?

11. Do you accept the differences there are between you both?

12. Do you want children? Does she?

13. Are you realistic about the baggage that either of you brings to your relationship?

14. Will you stick with her no matter what and work through problems which arise – even when you're both bored and overworked, overweight and overtired, undersexed and feeling undervalued?

15. Are you prepared for the big challenge of making your marriage the greatest success of your life?

Just happily married!

16. Does the thought of marriage make you nervous? (Good – that's means you understand the magnitude of your commitment, because divorce is not an option. If you are just going to give it your best shot and hope it works out – that won't be enough.)

17. What are the odds of your marriage being a success? The national average or 100 per cent?

18. Have you ever seen an old woman naked?

19. Are you still thinking about the last question?

20. Does it matter?

If you have any doubt about her answer then you don't know her – so don't propose.

How to Propose

It's been a perfect day. You've shared a bottle of champagne in the park, watched a movie and the sun going down and now you're holding hands with your beloved, strolling home a contented man.

....

You take a little black box from your pocket and your heart is beating so fast you think you're going to have an aneurysm. You drop to your knees and ask the question. She bleats with surprise 'Oh, oh, I can't believe it, yes, yes, of course I'll marry you, this is the happiest day of my life . . .'

Are you insane? Do you ever talk to each other? No one surprises their girlfriends like that any more and stays married for long. In the old days when men and women exchanged small talk instead of body fluids and married strangers, a proposal was a revelation. Nowadays, you should both know whether you plan to spend the rest of your lives together. You should have discussed it.

It needn't spoil the spontaneity. A proposal of marriage should be a special moment, not because she doesn't expect it, but because she doesn't know when or how you will propose. That's where the romance and originality come in.

If you have any doubt about her answer then you don't know her – so don't propose. Do you really want to marry someone you don't know?

You can make a public or private proposal – chosen with care to suit her personality. Don't put her on the spot in front of thousands of people unless you know she'll enjoy it. Again, you should know what she likes.

Public: On the radio, on TV, via the scoreboard during half time at a football match, hang a banner on the motorway, paint it on a roof and take her up in an aeroplane to read it . . .

Private: Just the two of you on top of a mountain, in a cable car, on the back of a yak in the Himalayas, swimming in the Caribbean, over a candlelit dinner, after making love . . .

Above all it should be personal. You must include elements that are significant to both of you, rather than copy the ideas of others. You could return to the place where you first met, or if she's passionate about horses or swimming with dolphins or eating pizza you'll know to include it in your plans. A book can't tell you how to propose. If you're in love and want to grow old together, you'll figure it out.

Signs she's about to Dump You

You're blissfully happy and seem really into each other. You like her a lot and think she feels the same way about you. Life is great until, without any warning, you have an argument and she's walked out of the door never to return.

....

You didn't see it coming. What went wrong? Was it something you did or didn't do? How can you stop it from happening again? These things don't occur overnight – they build up over several weeks or months. The signs are there. You need to know what to look out for so that next time you can take evasive action.

If you follow your gut feeling then you won't need to look for signs because you'll just know that something isn't quite right. But if you are fooling yourself, here are some clues to convince you that you should start paying attention to that knotted sensation in your stomach.

1. Her behaviour changes dramatically in a relatively short space of time.

2. Whenever you start talking about your future together she changes the subject or begins to get visibly uncomfortable.

3. Her behaviour may become secretive.

4. She starts farting in your face or leaves her tampons lying around.

5. She starts lying to you. Watch her eyes when she's explaining why she stayed out all night. If she looks to the left she is accessing the creative side of her brain, which means she may be telling porkies. If she won't look you in the eye or takes long pauses before speaking, she's fabricating an excuse.

6. If she has something to hide it will show in her body language, which will become closed or unusually static. She may be working so hard not to give anything away that she'll become unnaturally still.

7. She may start petty arguments or sulk a lot – classic passive-aggressive behaviour designed to get you to do her dirty work for her and initiate a separation.

8. She may start to take extra special care on her appearance, except it doesn't appear to be for your benefit. She's bought lots of new clothes, has lost weight and has taken out gym membership, but is unresponsive to your physical advances.

Don't turn your girlfriend into your therapist. In the early days of the relationship she may complain that you aren't opening up enough to her emotionally, but this doesn't mean that she wants to spend the rest of her life being your counsellor. You must still take ultimate responsibility for your emotions and learn to cope with all the things life throws at you, including getting dumped.

How to Dump Her Like a Gentleman

There's an old line which says that the reason divorce is so expensive is because it's worth it. If you're stuck in a relationship and you want out, be honest with yourself and her before you both walk down the aisle only to become yet another divorce statistic. If you're already married, then put some more effort into it, you slacker.

....

There's no getting away from the fact that men dump women (and vice-versa) because they're not happy with what they've got and may be looking for an upgrade. Not pretty, but there you have it. Either the grass is greener or your own grass is turning to straw. Maybe you want to experience life with as many different women as possible before you settle down with 'the one'. Or maybe you can't understand what you first saw in her and would rather be dating a mountain troll than spend another moment together.

Either way, you've got to dump her decisively with a fair degree of honesty. It won't be pretty. She may get angry and upset. Your job is to minimise the damage. You don't want her ending up in therapy or slagging you off to everyone she meets for the next five years. It's not really possible to let someone down gently. Break ups are painful if you care about each other.

First of all you must do it in person. Sending an email makes for a great story if you're trying to win a cyber-bastard award, but really if you don't break up face to face you're a coward.

The time has to be now. Don't postpone your own happiness. The longer you wait the more painful it will become, the more future plans will have to be broken and the more betrayed she will feel.

The other problem to consider by not taking the bull by the horns now is the disruption of future events. There will always be holidays, weddings, plans that need cancelling. If you wait until every future plan has been seen through you'll find yourself standing her up at the altar, or, worse still, getting married followed by a quick divorce.

#

Chances are she'll rebound into another guy faster than you find your dream woman.

Just be honest. Accept that a polite and friendly break-up is only likely if she feels the same way as you. Otherwise there will be tears and anger and flying insults. That's normal, though uncomfortable. If she starts crying hysterically, this will pass. She'll get over you and find someone else. Chances are she'll rebound into another guy faster than you find your dream woman.

The next time you see her she may have lost twenty pounds and appear independent and 'over you'. This is when you'll be at your most vulnerable. It's hard to bear when our women regain their independence after a break-up – it brings up the temptation and challenge of the chase all over again. You've chased her once, don't do it again. Whatever problems there were will always return.

Be as civil as you can be. Don't be cold – it feels more comfortable to pretend that you never felt anything for her. You want to convince her that it's over – but don't make her feel like the whole thing was a sham right from the start or she'll never trust another man again. If you told her you loved her and meant it, but now you don't love her, that doesn't mean you never loved her – so don't take that away from her too.

Choose the place where you break up carefully. If you meet in public she is less likely to cause a scene by bursting into tears. However, this could backfire, so if you break up in McDonalds you could have fifty people eating their burgers while you and your girlfriend provide the cabaret. If you meet in private, make sure it's somewhere you can leave. Don't ditch her at your flat because you will spend the next four hours trying to scrape her off your sofa.

Wait for a few weeks before playing the field again, otherwise word will get back to her that you're going at your new bachelorhood like a man possessed.

She will get over you. She may be inconsolable now – especially if young – you feel like she will spend the rest of her life recovering. However, it's better to do the damage now than be grey and unhappy.

Hasta la Vista, Baby.

Index